RECKLESS ENTANGLEMENT

IONA ROSE

Book #1
Hunter Bros

Hey there!

Thank you for choosing my book. I sure hope that you love it. I'd hate to part ways once you're done though. So how about we stay in touch?

My newsletter is a great way to discover more about me and my books. Where you'll find frequent exclusive giveaways, sneak previews of new releases and be first to see new cover reveals.

And as a HUGE thank you for joining, you'll receive a FREE book on me!

With love,

Iona

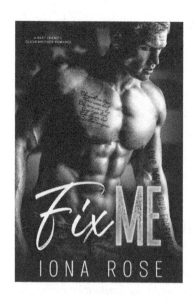

Get Your FREE Book Here:
https://dl.bookfunnel.com/v9yit8b3f7

Reckless Entanglement

Publisher: Some Books
ISBN- 9781913990169

Chapter One

CALLIE

I hurry across the parking lot, coming as close as I can to running without risking breaking an ankle. My skin tight pencil skirt and killer heels aren't the kind of outfit a girl runs in. They aren't the sort of outfit I ever pictured myself waitressing in either, but that's the joy of working in La Trattoria. I can't complain though. It's high end enough that the tips from my part time job pay my bills and leave me with enough time to study for college.

I check my watch as I burst through the back door and into the staff room, a grubby room filled with a scratched table and three broken chairs. A stark contrast to the restaurant floor where everything is immaculate, brand new and shiny.

My heart sinks when I see Marco sitting in one of the chairs, his feet propped up on the table. As bosses go, he's the worst. He's by far the laziest man I've ever met, but his standards rival those of The Waldorf when it comes to us waitresses. He makes a show of looking at his watch. He tuts and shakes his head.

"I'm sorry," I say, already taking my coat off. "There was an accident on the way in and the diversion was crazy busy. I'll make the time up I swear."

"See that you do Callie." He gets up and saunters towards the door, blocking my path as I try to leave the room. "This is just unprofessional. I guess I shouldn't expect better from a student though, huh?"

With that, he's gone, leaving me standing there open mouthed at the sheer audacity of him calling me unprofessional. All of this drama because I was two minutes late. Like *literally* two minutes. It's not really about me being a few minutes late though. It's about me rejecting his advances last week when he hit on me in his office.

As if I could ever be attracted to him. I mean he's not ugly or anything to look at, but boy is he ugly on the inside. Besides, sleeping with the boss is such a cliché, and I refuse to be one of those girls who is never quite sure if she's kept around because she's good at her job, or because she's eye candy for the boss.

I shake my head, telling myself to let it go. I won't let that douchebag into my head. I hit the restaurant floor with my fake smile plastered on.

"Callie? Table three is up," the line chef shouts the second I appear.

I rush forward and grab the two plates. They're hot, burning my skin and I almost let them go, but I manage to hold onto them. I'm used to being burned by the plates, but the first time each night always gets me. I rush them to the table, slowing down at the last second and smiling once more. "One carbonara?" I say.

The woman at the table smiles and gestures that it's hers.

I set the plate down in front of her and turn to the man. "And one lasagna." I smile, placing the plate down in front of him. "Enjoy your meals."

They thank me, but as I walk away, I can hear them muttering under their breath about how long it's taken. Great. That's hardly my fault, I wasn't even here when their order was taken, but it'll be me who gets stiffed on the tip.

As I rush back to the counter, Marco catches up with me. "Table three are not impressed with your service Callie, and frankly, neither am I. Get it together or you're done here," he says.

I bite my tongue, determined not to let him get to me. He knows that order being late wasn't my fault. Sasha, one of the other waitresses catches my eye and pulls a face behind Marco's back, making me feel slightly better about the whole thing.

I reach the counter and collect the next order, a single pizza. I turn around to deliver it and find Marco once more blocking my path.

"Are you ignoring me?" he demands.

"No," I say, nodding towards the plate in my hand. "Just trying to get us caught up."

"Maybe we wouldn't be in the weeds if you had shown up on time," he says, but he moves out of my way.

I can feel my temperature rising in anger at his tone of voice as I rush across the restaurant. My focus is on trying not to show my anger, and I'm not paying as much attention as I should be to the restaurant floor. Before I register what's happening, I feel myself tripping.

I start to fall and everything slows down as my stomach turns over. I have time to imagine the clatter as I slam to the ground, the laughter, Marco's anger that I've wasted the pizza. As if by a miraculous intervention warm hands catch the tops of my arms saving both me and the pizza from taking a dive.

I look up to thank my savior but the words die on my lips as I take in the tousled rich brown hair, the square jaw, and the deep chocolate eyes I could easily lose myself in. I swallow hard, dragging my eyes away hurriedly as I feel my cheeks turning red. My eyes move downwards of their own accord, taking in a black shirt covering huge pecs and abs of steel.

My stomach rolls again, but this time it's nothing to do with me falling. It's him. His hands are still on me and I can feel him watching me. I look back up to his face and once more I am assaulted by his eyes.

"For God's sake take the pizza to the damned customer," Marco hisses in my ear.

The moment is broken and the man pulls his hands away from me, although he still holds my gaze with his own. I try to thank him, but my voice is gone and I just scurry away, thanking my lucky stars that the table is one of the ones in the patio area.

The cool night air washes over me as I go outside and I feel the flush in my cheeks start to die down. I deliver the pizza uneventfully and take a moment to just breathe in a few deep breaths. I steel myself for Marco's tirade and head back inside.

A woman practically runs towards me when she sees me come back in. "I'm so sorry miss," she says. "Are you ok?"

"I-I'm fine," I say with no idea who she is or what's going on.

She sees confusion written all over my face and she smiles sheepishly. "It was my bag you tripped over," she explains.

"Oh," I say, forcing a soft laugh. "Don't worry about it. Really, I should have been watching where I was going." I excuse myself as soon as I can without looking rude and make my way back towards the counter.

"Chef wants you to go and grab some ice from out back," Sasha says as I approach.

I nod, glad for the chance to get off the floor and take a moment to compose myself. I've been here less than half an hour and my shift is already spiralling. I hurry out the back and I spot him again. The man who saved me. He's talking to Marco and my heart sinks for a moment. Is he complaining about me?

I realize with a start the shirt he's wearing isn't any old black shirt. It's one of ours. He must have started working here tonight. Great. So I have to see him every time I'm working now.

I've allowed myself to become distracted again, and as I walk, I kick a trash can, hurting my toes so badly I curse out loud before I can stop myself.

Marco and the hot guy both turn in my direction, but Marco might as well not be there. The guy's eyes are on mine again, and I can see the lust in them. It's like his eyes are burning through my clothes, stripping me naked.

I feel myself get wet at the thought of where his hands might go, where his tongue might go. I want to look away, but I can't. I am getting flustered, my skin flushing again, my heart racing and my palms sweating. He winks at me, a wink that sends a shiver through my body, and then he breaks eye contact and I can move again, think again.

"Callie, get over here," Marco shouts.

Oh, wonderful. Now he's going to embarrass me in front of the hot guy. Reluctantly, I head over. "Chef needs some ice," I explain.

"Chef can wait a moment," Marco says. "I want to introduce you to Matt. He's just transferred here from another branch. I want you to show him around, make him feel welcome. If that's not too much trouble." He walks away without another word.

I shake my head. "Asshole," I mutter under my breath.

"I hope you mean him and not me." Matt grins.

I nod, confirming it to be the case, but I'm not so sure I'm not talking about both of them. Matt is hot and there's no denying the effect he has on me, but no one should be this cool and arrogant on their first night in a new job.

Something tells me Matt is going to be trouble and I vow then and there that I will keep my distance from him. I'll show him the ropes, but that's it. I'll be cool and professional and leave it at that. I can do that. I can.

Chapter Two

MATT

"The break room and restroom is that way, and as you know the restaurant floor is that way," Callie says, pointing first one way and then the other.

I nod, watching her with amusement as she tries and fails to keep her eyes off my chest. I guess I'm not one to talk. From the moment she fell into my arms, I knew there was something special about her.

For starters, she's beautiful. Her eyes are a stunning, vivid green, the color of emeralds. Her skin is flawless and I want to reach out and run my fingers down her cheek. Her long gold-brown hair is pulled back into a high ponytail, but I can see how long it is and I can't help but imagine her pulling it loose, imagine myself pushing my hands into it, pulling her closer to me. My cock is getting hard just thinking about what I could do to this gorgeous creature.

I allow my eyes to move lower, taking in her full breasts, the curve of her hips. She sure knows how to rock this uniform like no one I've ever met.

She clears her throat and I know she's caught me staring. That makes two of us then. I meet her eyes and smile at her. "And my tour is over?" I say.

"I'm sorry. I have a lot to do. No offense Matt, but if you need hand holding, you're not going to last two minutes here," she says.

"Got it," I say, pushing myself up from the wall I've been leaning on. "Thank you for making me feel so welcome." I walk away, heading for the restaurant floor, grinning to myself. I don't need to look back to know that Callie is watching me walk away, her jaw hanging open in shock.

She's made it clear to me that her plan is to avoid contact with me as much as possible. It should raise my suspicions, yet strangely, it doesn't. I'm not blind. I saw the way she was looking at me. And I have a feeling that's why she wants to avoid me. Maybe she's one of those girls who don't date colleagues.

In one sense, I'm upset that Callie doesn't want to be around me. I would be more than happy to have her around me all day, every day. But in another sense, I think it's a good thing, because I can't allow my focus to slip, and at least this way, I don't have to be the one to push her away.

I'm here for one reason and one reason only, and that reason is too important to spend my time flirting with Callie. I came here to do what needs to be done. Not to make friends, and most certainly not to fall for one of the waitresses.

I'll play along with Callie's avoidance of me. That way, I can't become distracted from the real reason I'm here.

he walk for ice does me good. By the time I return with it to the kitchen, I've managed to push thoughts of Matt out of my mind altogether. I'm not thinking about his deep brown eyes. I'm not thinking about what I want him to do to me. I'm not thinking about that accent – my God that accent. Well ok, I'm thinking about Matt just a little bit, but I've also accepted that I'm going to stay well away from him.

His attitude makes me think he's a player and I just don't need that shit in my life. And if Marco got wind of anything happening between us, he would make my life hell. Like even worse than he makes it now. And I really don't need that.

I dump the ice out of the bags and head back to the restaurant floor. I manage to run a few tables without incident, and I'm starting to think that my bad luck has left me. They say it comes in threes. So I was late, I tripped and then I stubbed my toe on a trash can. So yeah, I've had my share of bad luck for the day.

As the rush begins to tail off and the restaurant moves at a more sedentary pace, Sasha makes her way over to me. "Who's the new guy?" she asks.

"His name's Matt," I say, careful to keep my voice neutral.

"Matt, right. Cute, isn't he?" she says.

"Sure," I reply. She would never buy it if I told her I hadn't noticed. No one with eyes would buy that, and especially not Sasha who knows me pretty well.

"You two might want to keep your distance from him," James, another waiter, says as he comes to join us.

"I'm a happily married woman." Sasha laughs. "It's only Callie you have to worry about."

I feel my face flush and I want to move the conversation onto something else, but James' words have me intrigued. "What makes you say that? You jealous because he's getting all of the attention?" I tease him.

"Actually, it's nice to have a break from all of the attention," James jokes. "Seriously though, I heard he's trouble. Rumor has it he's the youngest manager the chain has ever had. Twenty-four I heard. And he screwed up big time. That's why he's here. Got demoted and sent here as punishment I guess."

Sasha rolls her eyes. "God James, where do you get this shit from? I swear you're worse than us girls for gossiping. How much of that did you make up?"

"None of it, I swear," he says with a laugh.

"So who told you?" she demands.

"I have my sources," James says.

A man sitting at one of his tables catches James' eye and he scuttles away.

I turn to Sasha. "What have you heard?"

She shrugs. "Nothing much. You're the one who got the formal introduction. What did Marco tell you?"

"Just his name and that he's been transferred here from another branch. He only wanted me to show him around because he thought I'd get less done and he'd have another reason to berate me."

"You know what he's like. Don't let him get to you Callie. And to be fair, if that's your punishment, well I might start acting out myself." she laughs.

I laugh and shake my head. "Seriously though, it's probably not what James said. Surely, if he'd done something that bad, they'd just fire him. I guess we give Matt the benefit of the doubt until we get to know him."

"Yeah, I guess." Sasha nods.

The head chef calls from the counter and I hurry over to collect desserts for one of my tables. I know I told Sasha to give Matt the benefit of the doubt, and I meant it, but I can't help mulling over James' words. What he said would make sense. It would explain Matt's cocky arrogance. How he acted like he was above being a waiter. And it would explain why he seemed to be eyeing Marco with suspicion at one point. He could be jealous that Marco holds the job he threw away. Maybe his screw up wasn't quite bad enough to get fired for. They probably sent him to Marco on purpose, figuring after putting up with him for a week or two, he might quit of his own accord.

I shrug away the thoughts. It doesn't matter. Matt isn't my problem. And he's not going to become a problem. Knowing that he may have been a manager at one of our other branches actually makes me feel better, because I've pretty much left him to fend for himself since Marco told me to show him the ropes. If he's done the manager's job, in theory, he knows more about the ropes than I do.

I still feel a little guilty, but I let it go. I'm not going to get mixed up with Matt just because Marco wants it to happen. Screw Marco. It'll give him something to berate me over; something I've actually done rather than his personal grudge against me coming in to play.

The rest of my shift goes over without incident. My bad luck does seem to have come to an end and I've made a decent amount in tips. When my shift finishes, I feel kind of tired, it's been a busy one, but I also feel pretty good. When Marco isn't around, I enjoy my job, and I've barely seen him since he tried to palm Matt off onto me.

I go through to the break room and collect my things. I am just about to leave when Matt walks in. He smiles at me and I feel my heart flutter, but I tell myself to stop it. He's changed out of his uniform, he's wearing jeans and a plain white t-shirt that shows off his tanned, muscular arms, and gives me a hint as to how amazing his abs are underneath that t-shirt.

His smile seems genuine, and I don't want to be rude to him. There's a difference between keeping your distance and being outright mean, and I don't want to make anyone feel the way Marco makes me feel. "How was your first shift?" I ask.

"Good." He smiles. "Nice and busy. And I got through it with my uniform still clean, so that's a success right?"

"Right," I reply, feeling myself relaxing slightly. "Staying clean and not dropping anything is pretty much the best you can expect on your first night."

"I guess I did ok then." He's still smiling.

Better than me by all accounts, as I would have dropped a dish if Matt hadn't have caught me. I realize I still haven't thanked him for stopping me from face planting on the restaurant floor. "I never did thank you. For stopping me from going flying in the dining room earlier."

"You still haven't." His grin turns playful, making his eyes twinkle and my pussy clench. "You just pointed it out."

A laugh comes from my lips unbidden and I give him a playful shove, aware of the sparks that flood through my hand and up my arm as I touch him. "Thank you," I say. "There, I said it."

"And thank you for making my first night a success," he says.

I feel my cheeks redden. I deserved that. "I—"

"I'm serious Callie," he says, cutting me off. "You obviously know what you're doing here. It's sink or swim right? If you'd have had me shadow you, I'd be no further forward."

He thinks my complete avoidance of him was some sort of training technique? I'm happy enough to go along with that. It's a much better scenario than the one where I have to admit I'm avoiding him because I don't think I can control myself around him. Not that I'd ever admit it. I decide to move our conversation back onto safer ground. I nod towards the doors. "Are you ready to leave?"

He nods and I pull the door open. I step through and keep it open for him.

He steps out and thanks me.

"Which way are you heading?" I ask.

He nods in the general direction I'm going in to catch my train.

"Me too," I say.

We start to walk and I suddenly wonder if he thinks I'm just saying it, so we can spend a few extra minutes together. Surely, he won't think that. Like I'm hiding the fact I'd follow him pretty much anywhere. Just in case, I decide to clarify things. "I'm catching the 10:35 train," I say.

"Ah, me too," Matt says.

I raise an eyebrow. Is he following me? I wish.

"Whereabouts do you live?" he asks.

"Just a couple of stops away. I'm studying at the university. I have a dorm room there," I say. "What about you? You're not a student. I would definitely have noticed you around campus." I feel my cheeks heat up as I realize what I've said.

Matt gives me an amused smile. "I'm in Felton."

Again with the arrogant kind of smile that reminds me why I'm meant to be staying away from him. "Nice," I comment.

His expression changes for a moment, a look of regret crossing his face, like he shouldn't have told me where he lives.

The look is gone before I can truly register it and I tell myself I'm being paranoid. There was no look.

I can easily picture someone like Matt living in Felton. Felton isn't the sort of neighborhood girls like me live in. It's an elite place, where the houses are situated seemingly miles apart from each other, each one planted in the middle of an extensive garden. What I can't work out is what the fuck someone who lives on an estate like that is doing working as a waiter.

I refused to acknowledge the part of me that warms inside at his words, the part that is excited to know I'll be spending the whole train journey in his company. We arrive at the station just as the train pulls in. "Perfect timing," I say.

"Indeed," Matt says, giving me a look I can't quite read.

We get onto the train, Matt gesturing at me to get on first. I take a window seat and silently pray that Matt sits beside me. He does. I tell myself it means nothing. How could he sit anywhere else without looking like a total jerk? That doesn't stop my heart from racing too fast as I feel his leg pressing against mine. My stomach whirls, my clit throbbing. I am eager for more of his touch, a touch more intimate.

I clear my throat and look out of the window for a moment, trying to slow my heart rate down.

"Is the station that interesting or am I that boring?" Matt asks after a couple of seconds.

I turn back to him, shaking my head. "Neither. I thought I saw someone I knew, that's all," I lie.

"Well, it's good to know you don't think I'm boring." He winks.

"Ah... I didn't exactly say that did I?" I tease him. "I don't know enough about you to decide that yet."

The train gives a whistle and pulls slowly out of the station, picking up speed.

"We'll have to see what we can do about that then." Matt nods. "I'd hate for your thrilling commute to become boring."

I bite my lip to stop myself from blurting out what's in my head; the commute is already a hundred times more exhilarating than any other train journey I've ever taken. I am saved from embarrassing myself when the ticket collector comes to our seat, asking to see our tickets.

I pull mine from my jacket pocket and he takes it and stamps it. Matt asks for a single to Felton and pays the conductor. I wonder briefly how he got to work if not on the train, but I don't ask. He could have caught a bus, or been dropped off by a friend. It's not suspicious and I need to stop trying to make Matt out to be some sort of fucking James Bond.

The ticket inspector moves on and Matt turns back to me. "So the more I think about it, the more you've convinced me that I am actually pretty boring," he says. "I had a normal childhood with normal parents and normal siblings. And now I'm a normal waiter in a normal restaurant. There is one thing though, something I try to keep quiet, but you seem like someone I can trust." He looks around, beckoning me closer.

I hold my breath, waiting for his big secret. I'm nervous suddenly, unsure of what he's about to reveal.

Lowering his voice he says, "Sometimes, if we have a family meal and no one is looking, I take the last roasted potato."

I throw my head back and laugh, surprised at how easily he was able to reel me in.

He laughs with me, enjoying my reaction.

"You're a bad man." I laugh. "Everyone knows the last potato is off limits."

"I'm a monster," he confirms. "But not boring right?"

"Right," I agree as I chuckle.

We chat some more and I begin to see the real Matt, the person beneath the cool and arrogant exterior. He's warm and funny, so I find myself relaxing completely in his company. He still has a profound effect on me, the intensity of his gaze, the way he rests his hand on my knee for a second as we laugh, but it seems more genuine now. I realize he's not arrogant at all. His humor is mostly self-deprecating and I think his arrogance is most likely a front he puts up to appear more confident than he is.

All too soon, my stop approaches. I'm not ready for this to be over. I'm doing the worst job of avoiding Matt, but now I've seen a different side to him, I have to wonder if I should even want to keep my distance from him. "This is me," I say, as the tinny voice announces my upcoming stop.

Matt stands up and lets me pass. "Are you working tomorrow?" he asks me.

"Yeah. I'm on the closing shift all week. You?"

"Same," he says.

The train pulls to a stop and I make for the doors.

"So I guess I'll see you tomorrow, Callie."

I can't help but feel a shiver run through my body as I step off the train and feel Matt's eyes on me, watching me across the station.

Chapter Four

MATT

I watch Callie until she's out of sight. The second she moves through the turnstiles and off the platform, I jump to my feet and run for the doors, making it through just in time before they hiss closed. I move in the opposite direction to where I've seen Callie disappear from sight. I slip into the men's room and go into a cubicle, locking the door. I have to make sure she's out of sight before I leave the station. I don't want to risk her turning around and seeing me.

I stand in the cubicle, trying my best not to touch anything and not to breathe too deeply. It's not exactly clean and I don't want to spend a minute longer here than I have to, but sometimes, needs outweigh everything else and this is one of those times.

I keep looking at my watch, waiting for ten minutes to pass. Each minute feels like an hour, and I give up after five minutes and leave. I go back out onto the platform, glad to be able to take a deeper breath. I leave the station and pull my phone out of my jeans pocket. I make a quick call and arrange to be picked up from the station.

I lean my back against the wall and wait, my mind going back to Callie. I smile to myself as I hear her musical laughter in my mind. I love being able to make her laugh, love thinking I could maybe make her happy.

But it's a road I can't afford to go down. I can't let myself get emotionally attached to Callie. It will only distract me from the real reason I'm here. I thought it was going to be easy to avoid getting attached to her. Although my cock hardened at the sight of her, and I pictured myself licking her all over, she showed no interest in me. In fact, after the initial moment where her piercing gaze took my breath away, she seemed like she could barely tolerate me.

I figured I could relax a little, maybe even have a bit of fun flirting with her. But then, she started to flirt back, and I came to see that the way she makes me feel is not one sided. That makes it harder. Much harder.

What I wouldn't have given to take her home with me, show her who I really am and fuck her all night long. I can't do that though. I can't let her in.

I shake my head a little, trying to push the thoughts of Callie from my mind. I have to be focused on the task at hand. I tell myself there will be no more flirting. I'll be friendly to Callie, but that's it. Anything else is off the table. No matter how hard keeping it that way might turn out to be.

Chapter Five

CALLIE

hings seem to have changed between Matt and me. After that first day, where the chemistry between us was sizzling hot, I went into work the next day expecting, well I'm not entirely sure what I was expecting. Something. Something very different than what I got.

It felt like Matt had put up a wall. Not a wall to keep me out entirely, but a wall that said our flirtations and the chemistry between us was out of bounds. He went from being the hot stranger to the guy I shared the train ride home with and somehow, somewhere over the week, I started to think of him as a friend.

We were scheduled on the closing shift together, and each night we were the only two left by the time we pulled the shutter down on the restaurant. Technically, as I had been there longer, I was the senior member of staff, but Matt took the job of performing the nightly security checks seriously and I let him do it.

We'd catch the train every night and laugh and joke and tease each other on the way home until my stop rolled around. I had managed to convince myself that I wasn't attracted to Matt. It wasn't entirely true, but I'd gotten what I wanted. A way to avoid the obvious chemistry between us and the complications of dating someone I worked with.

The first night we were alone together, my stomach was a rolling pit of need. I kept thinking Matt would try to kiss me. I kept asking myself whether or not I'd let him if he did. Tonight, there's no such thought in my mind as I say goodbye to the last table of stragglers and close the door behind them. I lock it and turn to Matt, pressing my back to the door and wiping fake sweat from my brow.

He laughs at my theatrics.

I grab the mop from him. "You go and grab our stuff and check the back door and I'll finish up the last bit of floor," I say.

"Yes, boss," he says, snapping off a salute.

I shake my head as he leaves the restaurant floor. I can't help but watch the way his ass ripples inside of his trousers as he strides across the floor. I mean there's no harm in looking right? He moves out of sight and I quickly wipe down the last table and finish the floor. I empty the mop bucket out and just as I'm pulling the cleaning supplies cupboard door closed, Matt appears.

He smiles and holds out my coat. I slip it on and he hands me my bag. "Ready?" he asks.

"More than ready," I reply.

We lock up and set off towards the station.

"Have you got any plans for the weekend?" Matt asks.

"I'm going to a party tomorrow night," I say. "Then Saturday I'll spend hungover and dying, then I'm back to work Saturday night. I honestly can't believe I've got tomorrow night off. You have no idea how many parties and events I've had to miss because Marco seems determined to ruin my social life by having me chained to the restaurant every weekend night."

"Maybe he just wants a pretty face to pull the crowds in on a weekend." Matt grins.

I playfully slap his arm, although my cheeks color at his compliment. "Don't let the other waitresses hear you say that." I laugh.

"Oh, I won't. I don't particularly need a lawsuit right now," he says.

"Maybe next week?" I laugh.

"Yeah, maybe. I'll check my planner and see if I have an opening." He chuckles.

"What about you? Do you have plans?" I ask.

"No," he says. "I expected to be working being the new guy and all that. Mind you, I'm in for a double shift Saturday and the same again Sunday, so it's not like I'm getting off easily."

"Ouch," I say.

"Yeah exactly," he agrees.

The train arrives and we get on then show the inspector our tickets.

"So tell me about this drunken college party," Matt asks as the inspector walks away.

"Well, it's pretty much as you described it. Our dorm parties usually get broken up pretty quickly, but this one is being thrown by a friend of mine who is in a house share off campus. He only has one neighbor and they're away for the weekend, so I reckon this one might last past eleven."

"Make sure it doesn't go past twelve though," Matt warns. "I'd hate to hear you'd turned back into a pumpkin."

"I think the story goes that Cinderella turns back into a slave girl and her carriage becomes a pumpkin," I say.

"Same thing." He shrugs.

"Besides, it wouldn't be the first time I'd left a party with only one shoe," I say. "But strangely, no prince has ever come to bring me the other one."

"I'm pretty sure that's the difference between magic and tequila shots." Matt laughs.

"Oh, I think they're pretty much one and the same. Both of them make me a wicked dancer." I laugh.

"Now I'm intrigued," Matt says as he jumps to his feet and gestures for me to get up into the aisle.

"What are you doing?" I hiss, aware that the people around us are staring.

"Waiting for you to show me your moves," he says.

"Ah, well there's definitely no magic on board and I haven't had my tequila I'm afraid." I giggle.

"Chicken." Matt laughs, sitting back down.

"You should come. To the party I mean," I say, feeling brave suddenly.

"I don't know. I think I might be a bit old for a college party."

"Yeah. I mean you're what twenty-five? You're ancient," I tease.

"Hey, less of the ancient" He laughs. "And actually I'm only twenty-four."

"So is that a yes then?" I push him.

"I..."

His tone of voice tells me he's about to say no, and suddenly, the thought of not seeing him tomorrow makes me feel a little lonely. "Now who's the chicken?" I interrupt him.

"Oh, I'll be there." He nods. "And this dancing thing? It's on."

"Oh it's on alright." I laugh, feeling a warm glow inside of me. I take Matt's number, telling him I'll text him the address, and when my stop rolls around, I get off the train feeling like I'm walking on air. Did I just ask Matt on a date and got a yes?

No... I caution myself. *You invited a friend to come to a party with you and he had nothing better to do so he agreed. That's all. Don't go getting any ideas.*

I think it might be a little bit too late for that though.

Chapter Six

CALLIE

"*L*et's go and get another drink," Chloe, my best friend, shouts over the thumping music.

I nod my agreement and let her lead me through the crowd. The party is in full swing. The living room and dining room are crammed full of people, some swaying to the music, some standing around the edges of the room chatting. The furniture has all been pushed back, leaving plenty of room for dancing. The room is hot and sweaty and it's getting more and more humid by the minute as more bodies squeeze in.

The stairs are littered with couples hooking up and I dread to think what's going on in the bedrooms if what I see on the stairs is anything to go by. Chloe leads me into the kitchen. The music is quieter there and the temperature is cooler. We make our way to the fridge which is empty of everything except bottles and bottles of beer.

Chloe grabs two and looks around for the bottle opener. She finds it and hands a bottle to me, keeping the other for herself. "Will you cheer up," she laughs. "You're acting like you're here against your will or something. It's a party Callie, not a damned funeral."

"I'm sorry," I say, forcing a smile onto my face. "I'm just thinking about how ill I'm going to feel tomorrow at work."

It's a lie. Well no, it's not entirely a lie. I will be ill at work tomorrow and I'll curse myself for tonight, but that's not why I'm miserable. I'm miserable because Matt hasn't shown up. It's after nine and I figured if he was coming he'd have been here by now. Or at least, he would have text me to let me know he was planning on coming soon.

"Tomorrow's another day." Chloe grins. "Now drink and see if that will put a smile on your face."

I take a long drink from the bottle, telling myself to forget about Matt and just enjoy the party. It's not fair to Chloe for me to be so damned miserable and I don't want to ruin the party for her. "Shots," I say, moving to a table filled with shots of vodka Jello.

I grab a blue one and an orange one and hand Chloe the orange one. She winces, but she takes it. We peel the lids off the shots and tip our heads back. I feel the too big lump of Jello slide over my tongue and I try to chew it and straighten my head up at the same time. I end up choking out a cough as the Jello shot remains in my throat. My cough easily dislodges it, and I start to chew again. I feel like a damned hamster. My cheeks are that full.

Chloe, who has somehow gotten through her Jello as easily as if it were liquid, laughs at me.

Her laughter sets me off and although I try to bite it back, I can't. I make a snorting sound and Jello bits run from my mouth as the laughter bursts out of me. I shake my head, looking away from Chloe whose laughter is only making mine more pronounced. As I turn my head to the side, I come face to face with Matt.

Fuck.

"Classy lady." He smiles at me.

I try to frantically wipe the Jello off my chin but I still have a wad of it stuck in my mouth which I chomp down on twice and force myself to swallow hoping for the best.

Chloe looks from me to Matt and back to me again.

I can read her expression. *He's cute. Go for it.*

"You made it," I say to Matt when I finally get the Jello down.

"Yeah. Just in time for your show by the looks of it." He laughs.

"Ah, you should see my encore." I grin.

Chloe is still watching us, clearly annoyed that I haven't told her about Matt. "I'm Chloe, Callie's best friend when it suits her," she says, sticking her hand out.

"Matt," Matt says, shaking her hand. "And why only when it suits her?"

"Well, she didn't tell me she had a date tonight," Chloe says.

I feel my cheeks flushing. I open my mouth to correct her, but I'm too slow, and she keeps talking, making me more mortified with every word.

Matt watches her with amusement, revelling in my discomfort.

"At least now that you're here, she's smiling. And it explains why she's been so miserable all night. Hangover my ass."

"So Matt, did you find the place ok?" I interject quickly. My voice is too loud and my question is too lame, but I had to say something. I had to stop Chloe's verbal diarrhea.

"Yeah, pretty easy actually." Matt nods. "I just followed the sound of the music and the shrieking."

"I'm going to go catch up with Lou," Chloe says. "I'll be around." She walks away, giving me a thumbs up as she leaves the kitchen.

"She's subtle isn't she?" Matt jokes.

"Oh, you have no idea," I laugh. "This is Chloe on her best behavior." I realize, too late, that I never did correct her about Matt being my date. The way he's attracting the attention of the girls who wander in and out of the kitchen, I think maybe that's a good thing.

"Are you ready to show me these moves of yours then?" Matt smiles. "Or did I come here under false pretenses?"

"Well I would, but there's no tequila here," I joke.

"Funnily enough, I thought you might say that." Matt winks. He reaches into the inside pocket of his black leather jacket and pulls out a small bottle of tequila. "And now there is."

"Jackpot!" I grin. "After one of those, just you try and stop me from showing you my moves."

He smiles at me and opens the bottle. He takes a swig and winces as he swallows. He holds the bottle out to me.

I take it and my fingers brush his. I ignore the sparks that fly as our fingers touch. It's just the beer I tell myself, although I know for a fact that's not entirely true. I bring the bottle to my lips, very much aware that just seconds ago, Matt's lips where on the exact spot mine are now touching. I take a drink from the bottle, shuddering as the liquid burns my mouth. I swallow and quickly chase it down with a long drink of beer. It hits my stomach and begins to warm my insides.

I feel brave suddenly, whether it's the tequila, the party atmosphere, or the sparks I felt when Matt's fingers touched mine I don't know, but I grab Matt's hand and start to lead him out of the kitchen and into the living room area. I drag him to the makeshift dance floor, and just as we arrive, one of my favorite songs comes on. I shriek and Matt laughs.

We start to dance and I feel myself relax. My relaxed state doesn't last very long as Tiffany, a girl from the year above me at college comes sidling over. She not so casually slips herself between me and Matt and begins to shake her hips, pretending not to have noticed she's pushed me out.

I feel an irrational surge of anger flood through me, and it takes a lot for me to not reach out and shove her back to wherever the fuck she came from. One more shot of tequila and I might just have done that. The anger in me at being shoved aside tells me one thing; I can tell myself all I like that Matt and I are just friends, but I want more.

Even as we became friends, I knew he was attractive, but it's only now that it hits me how much I desire him. I'm still trying to work out what to do about Tiffany without looking like a crazy, jealous bitch, when Matt solves the problem for me. He neatly side steps around Tiffany and I shift my position so that we're back dancing together.

"Are all of your friends that rude?" Matt shouts over the music.

I know Tiffany can hear him, and I know she will be able to hear my answer, "Only when they see a hot piece of ass."

Matt throws his head back and laughs as Tiffany stalks away from us.

As we dance, I look around and I can't help but notice the appreciative stares Matt is getting. No one else is quite as brazen as Tiffany, but there are a lot of girls here who would kill to be where I am right now.

Again, I feel that irrational anger inside of myself, only now, I recognize it for what it is. I'm jealous. I'm afraid that one of these girls is going to take Matt away from me. I mean we're just friends. He would have every right to hook up with someone if he wanted to. I guess I'll just have to make sure that someone is me.

I start to sway my hips a little more, and I run my hands over my dress as I dance, pressing it tightly against my body. I can feel Matt's eyes on me, his gaze following my hands as I move them. I pretend not to notice, pretend I barely know he's there, that I'm lost in the music.

I feel a hand slip into mine, and before I know it, Matt spins me away from him. He keeps a tight grip on my hand, extending his arm, and then he pulls me back in. I crash against his chest, our bodies mash together, and he doesn't let me go. He wraps his arms around my waist.

Nervous now, I tentatively wrap my arms around his shoulders. As we sway, I am conscious of Matt's solid chest pressed against mine. His strong arms pin me in place, his body wrapped around me. I can smell his aftershave and beneath it, the scent of his skin, musky and exotic. I breathe in deeper, enjoying the scent. I can feel my pussy responding to how close we are. I am so wet I can feel my panties dampening, sticking to my skin.

Matt's face is pressed close to mine, his cheek touching my own and I can hear him humming softly to the music. His breath tickles my neck, sending goose bumps down my body and I find myself wishing we were alone.

The song ends all too quickly and I go to move away from him. He lets me back up enough, we're face to face, but he doesn't release his grip on my waist. I can see the desire I feel for him reflected in his eyes. I swallow hard, my throat suddenly dry and my palms sweaty. I can hear my pulse pounding through my body and I feel my cheeks start to flush.

"The tequila was definitely a good idea," Matt says.

I nod in agreement, not trusting myself to speak as I lose myself in his eyes. He reaches up with one hand and tucks a loose strand of hair behind one of my ears. He moves his hand away slowly, running his fingers over my cheek, a caress that sends shivers through me.

He leans closer to me, closing the gap between us. My stomach whirls, my pussy clenches. This is it. We're going to kiss. Before his lips can meet mine, a hand touches his arm and he glances down to see who it belongs to.

"Don't I know you from somewhere," a girl asks him.

A girl I don't recognize. She's smoking hot though and I feel a sinking sensation in my stomach. She must be someone he's hooked up with before. And there's no way in hell I can compare to her.

Matt barely glances at her before he shakes his head. "No, sorry. You must have me mixed up with someone else."

"Oh. Sorry," the girl says and she moves away from us, clearly not quite convinced as she keeps glancing back at Matt.

I realize I can hear the music pounding out again, see the people dancing all around us, but when Matt was leaning in to kiss me, it all went away. It was just the two of us in our own little bubble. Now though, the moment has passed, the magic gone, and I'm just standing awkwardly in his arms. He seems to come out of the daze at the same moment as I do and we move our arms from around each other at the same time. He gives an awkward sounding cough.

I have to rescue the situation. "It's kind of hot in here," I shout. "Do you need some air?"

He nods and takes my hand in his to lead me through the crowd. I cringe inside as I think of how my sweaty hand must feel to him, but he makes no move to pull away and I relax. If he asks, I'll tell him it's condensation off my drink and hope he doesn't realize I'd left it in the kitchen when we went to dance.

We finally get through the crowd and head through the kitchen then out of the double doors onto the patio.

The cool night breeze envelopes me, and I take a few deep breaths. I really was too hot in there, although I think most of that was due to being so close to Matt.

A few people mill around the patio, but Matt doesn't stop there. He leads me off the patio and away from the house, down to the garden where it's quieter.

"So who was that girl? A hook up?" I ask, keeping my tone light.

Matt laughs and shakes his head. "Honestly, I have no idea who she was. I really think she had me confused with someone else." He pauses and when he speaks again, his tone is teasing, "Someone might think you're jealous, Callie."

I laugh, but I don't deny it.

"You don't have to worry. She's not my type," he adds.

Was I worrying? Yeah, I guess I was. I thought I was hiding it better than that though. "Well maybe, if you told me anything about yourself, I'd know." I smirk. I seem to tell Matt every little detail of my life, but I know very little about him.

"If I told you I'd have to kill you though, and that's kind of messy and I like this shirt," he says.

I raise an eyebrow at him.

"Fine," he says. "I'm a Russian spy."

"No accent," I tell him.

He purses his lips. "I'm a vampire."

"Nope. I've seen you walk in the sun."

"I'm an exotic prince from a foreign land, coming to find a bride."

"You catch the train every day. You expect me to believe you're royalty?"

"I'm just Matt, a waiter, who would much rather hear everything about the beautiful girl by his side than bore her with the details of his life."

"Oh, you smooth talker." I laugh, but I flush at his compliment. I know he's purposely avoiding my question, finding ways not to talk about himself, but in that moment, when I look up at him and feel my pussy clench, I don't care. I don't want us to end up arguing. I just want to enjoy the moment, my hand in his, our bodies close together as we walk.

We reach the end of the garden and Matt points out a wooden bench behind a fountain that stands off to one side of the garden. We walk to it and sit down. He moves closer to me as we sit, and I can feel his leg resting against mine. I want more than anything for him to just kiss me already.

"Tell me the dream." Matt smiles at me. "If you could go anywhere, do anything, what would it be?"

Right now, it would be for him to kiss me, touch me, take me home and make me scream his name as I come, but that's not a story I'm about to share. Instead, I revert back to the idea the teenage version of me thought up. An idea part of me would still like to pursue but probably never will. "I'd be in Japan, teaching English to children." I smile.

He smiles back at me. "Why Japan?"

"At school, we did a big project about Japanese culture. I was instantly fascinated by it all."

"But aren't you studying business rather than teaching?" he asks me.

I feel a warmth inside of me. He remembered what I'm studying. I nod and shrug. "Yeah. Business is practical, but you were talking about dreams." I notice as I'm talking that Matt is focused on my lips. I can see that look in his eyes again; the look that tells me the way I'm feeling isn't one sided.

He's watching my lips like he wants to taste them, his tongue licking over his own lips.

Before I can stop myself, I'm leaning in closer to him. My heart is pounding. I'm moving in for a kiss, and I'm suddenly terrified that Matt will laugh at me.

He doesn't though. Instead, he starts to lean in towards me as well.

I am so wet, so ready for this. I need to kiss him like I've never kissed anyone before. I need to kiss him in a way that says take me home and fuck me all night long. Our lips are almost touching, and I close my eyes. Matt's lips graze mine so gently I could convince myself I imagined the touch if it wasn't for the way my lips tingle.

Before he can deepen the kiss I long for, his phone rings. My eyes fly open as he jumps away from me as though I've burned him.

"Dammit," he shouts. He seems angry to have been disturbed, but he shrugs apologetically and moves away from me, pulling his phone out of his pocket and taking the call.

I am so fucking frustrated. It's like fate is stopping us from kissing. Twice it's almost happened, and twice we've been stopped.

I'm a little annoyed at Matt too, if I'm being honest. He couldn't very well have ignored the girl in the party without looking like a major dick, but he could have ignored the call. He could have waited until after we'd kissed and then called them back.

He's only gone for three or four minutes, and when I see him coming back, I'm determined to put aside my annoyance, laugh off the interruption, and pick back up where we started. One look at Matt's expression tells me that's not going to happen.

"I'm sorry Callie, I have to go," he says to me.

I can hear the genuine regret in his voice and for a moment, my own disappointment takes a back seat, overpowered by concern for him. I stand up and touch his arm. "Is everything okay? Has something happened?" I ask.

"Yeah everything's okay. Just... something came up. I'm sorry, I really do have to go ... see you tomorrow." The hint of regret has gone from his voice, leaving it a little cold and expressionless, and he turns and walks away from me without any further explanation. He doesn't even wait for an answer.

"Yeah, bye then," I say under my breath as I watch him walk back to the patio and into the house.

He doesn't look back once and I feel lost suddenly. In that moment, I know. I don't just like Matt. I don't just want a wild night with him. It's more than that. I've developed feelings for him. Feelings that are all too close to love — feelings that he clearly doesn't share.

I sit back down on the bench, feeling the cold I didn't notice before seeping into my bones. I bite my lip, forcing myself to hold back the tears that threaten to spill down my cheeks. I take a few deep breaths, then I stand up and hold my head up high.

Fuck this.

I'm not going to sit out here crying over some guy who clearly doesn't want me. I'm going to go back into the party and have the night of my life. I'm going to show myself I don't need Matt here to have a good time.

They're the right thoughts for me to have, I know that. Now I just need to find a way to make myself believe them. I have a heavy heart when I walk back into the party, but I force myself to put a smile on my face and at least look like I want to be there.

Chapter Seven

CALLIE

I walk out of my lecture, a lecture about direct marketing that I've barely heard a word of, with my head down, trying not to catch anyone's eye. I'm really not in the mood for polite conversation, or any conversation for that matter. I just want to head back up to my dorm room and hide away until it's time for work. Not that I particularly want to go there either. In fact, that will no doubt be worse than here. At least in class, I can be miserable if I want to. At work, I have to plaster on that smile and pretend like everything is just fucking awesome all the damned time.

Well, it isn't. It isn't at all.

"Hey, I know it's a Monday, but is there really any need for that expression?" Chloe asks as she comes up from behind me and slips her arm through mine.

I force myself to smile. I think for a second about the irony of it all. How I'm meant to be allowed to be miserable here and already, just seconds after thinking it, I'm wearing my work smile. "I was just thinking," I finally reply.

"Bullshit," Chloe replies. "Something's wrong. You think I don't know when your smile is fake? I swear, looking at it, I wonder how you keep a job working with people all day. And I know this mood has something to do with that guy at the party on Friday. We're going to go and grab a coffee and you're going to tell me all about it."

"I don't want to talk about it," I say shaking my head.

I told her this same thing on Friday at the party when she tried to coax it out of me there, and nothing has changed. If I didn't pour my heart out to her when I was drunk, I'm certainly not going to do it now, when I'm sober.

"I don't remember asking if you *wanted* to talk about it," Chloe says. She pauses, making an exaggerated pout and scratching her head. "Nope. I definitely didn't ask."

I open my mouth to tell her to back off, but she interrupts me.

"You clearly need to get this out, but if you don't want to, fine. We're still going for coffee though. And we can talk about something different."

We head down to the cafeteria. It's quiet as most of the students have finished their last lectures for the day and are heading home. Lucky them. Maybe they didn't get cornered, or maybe they know how to say no and mean it. Apparently, I haven't mastered that one yet.

We get our coffees and Chloe leads me to a table tucked away in the corner. "So what do you want to talk about?" she asks. "I know. I'll tell you about my day. Dr Herbert was away today and his lab assistant took over my lecture. Boy, is he hot. I have no idea what he was talking about, but he was so pretty to watch. And..."

Chloe's right. I do need to get this out. And I know her tactics. She'll go on like this about any old shit until she breaks me. That's how she works. And it's why it's actually harder to resist spilling my guts to her when I'm sober. Drunk me can follow her babbling and laugh along with her. Sober me will do just about anything to cut it off. "I think he might be married," I blurt out.

"Dr Herbert's lab assistant?" She frowns.

"No. Matt."

"Matt as in, hot Friday night party guy?"

I nod and look down into my coffee cup.

"What makes you think that?" she asks.

I find myself telling her everything. How Matt just kind of appeared in my life. How he was flirty and definitely giving me the come on, but then how he changed and became more of a friend. Finally, I tell her about how at the party, we almost kissed and then he got that phone call. The one that made him run away from me.

Chloe raises an eyebrow when I'm done. "And that's it? You've decided he's married because of one phone call?"

"It's not so much the call. It's the fact he took it when we were so close to kissing. And then the way he ran from me straight after it. It was like he'd let himself forget he had a wife, and then she called him, and he realized what he had been about to do," I tell her.

She considers this, blowing on the surface of her coffee and then taking a sip. "It could be that I guess. But it could also be one of a thousand other things. Maybe he got a call to say someone in his family had taken ill."

That would explain why he hadn't showed up for work for the last two days. But it wouldn't explain why he hadn't so much as texted me. "So why didn't he just tell me that?"

"I don't know." Chloe shrugs. "I might be way off base, but I'm just saying you should at least give him the benefit of the doubt until you know for sure one way or the other. Have you tried actually asking him?"

I shake my head. "No. He hasn't texted or called me and I'm not going to be that desperate girl who texts him first." It sounds petty when I say it out loud, but it makes sense in my head. Matt seems like the kind of guy who is used to girls chasing him, and I refuse to be just another desperado in the queue to bed him. I have a little bit more self-respect than that.

"Right. Sorry. I forgot we were living in the 1800s," Chloe says. "Oh, wait! We're not."

I sigh and shake my head. "Look I know it sounds stupid, but I can't just text him and accuse him of cheating on the wife I'm not certain he has can I?"

"Not if you're afraid of the answer. Anyway, don't you work with him? I mean you can ask around at work," she says.

"That's the thing. He doesn't really talk about himself. No one at work knows a thing about him."

"A man of mystery. I like it." Her eyes shine as she leans in closer. "So maybe he's not married. Maybe he's a hit man and he got the call for his next job."

"If you're not going to be serious about this, then why are we even having this conversation?" I try to sound stern but I can feel my lips twitching and I can't stop myself from laughing.

Chloe grins at me. "Ask him at work. Just put it out there, Callie. You deserve better than some cheating rat."

I bristle at her description of Matt. It's so far from the warm, funny guy I've gotten to know over the last week or so. Maybe I have gotten this all wrong. "That's the other thing. He hasn't shown up for work all weekend. He was scheduled for double shifts on Saturday and Sunday. He didn't show up for either of them."

"Ah, so that's what this is really about." Chloe smirks. "You're pissed off because you had to pick up his slack."

"I can't say I'm overly happy about it. You know Marco, my boss, hasn't even been trying to call him to find out where he is? He'll come swanning back in when he's ready and nothing will get said. If one of the other wait staff did that, we'd be out the door."

"What makes you so sure he won't be?"

"Well, when he is there, he does very little work. He tends to spend too long chatting with the customers, charming them. But he doesn't do much in the way of actually waiting on them. Marco doesn't say anything to him, but he lectures the rest of us about keeping up."

"Maybe Marco has himself a little man crush." Chloe laughs. "At least that would mean that Marco's moved on from hitting on you."

A shiver of revulsion goes through me as I remember being called to Marco's office. His disgusting little hand on my knee. The things he said to me. "That's true. I'd rather be in his bad books than in his *might want to sleep with me* books. But I still think it's wrong how Matt shirks everything and we're the ones taking the shit for it."

Chloe laughs and shakes her head.

"What?" I demand.

"Isn't it obvious?" she asks me.

I shake my head. I have no idea what she's talking about.

"You're not pissed off with Matt because he gets one over on Marco. You would totally celebrate that. You're pissed off because you want him and he hasn't called you quickly enough for your liking."

"That's not true," I say, too quickly. *Oh God. Is it true? Am I that far gone that I'm projecting my feelings about Matt rejecting me onto something else?*

"Whatever you need to tell yourself to get through the day Callie." Chloe smirks knowingly.

Dammit. I knew I shouldn't have let her draw me into this conversation. I should have just gone back to my dorm room like I'd planned to. Or listened to her go on about whatever it was. "Let's pretend for a second that you're right. And you're not by the way. What the hell do I do? Matt's made it pretty clear he doesn't want to talk to me, and if he turns back up at work, I have to face him."

"He might think you're the one that made that clear. Picture the scene. He gets a call that his dear grandad has been taken to hospital. He can't tell you because he's afraid he won't be able to get the words out without crying, and he doesn't want you to see him crying. So he leaves, hoping you call him later. But you don't. And so he thinks he's pissed you off and it's too late to explain. He now thinks you don't want to talk to him. Awww... poor Matt. It's all just a misunderstanding. If only he knew." Chloe shakes her head sadly, speaking like a voice over in a soap opera recap.

I can't help but laugh. She's so dramatic. "Ok, nice story. But seriously, Chloe. What do I do?"

"Well, you have two choices. You confront him, or you let this whole cloud you have hanging over you go and avoid him like the plague."

I think back to his first day on the job. I had managed to avoid him easily enough. I know I can do it again. The thing is, I don't want to. But Chloe's right. I can't go on in this limbo, and I'm not about to march up to Matt and embarrass myself by demanding to know why he didn't kiss me on Friday. What if he's not married and he just realized it was a bad idea? I don't think I could handle him laughing in my face and saying the tequila wore off.

"Avoid him it is then," I state with a nod.

Chloe shakes her head. "A beer says it doesn't happen." She grins.

"You're on." I grin back.

Chapter Eight

CALLIE

It's Thursday before Matt shows back up to work. Marco greets him like nothing has happened when he strolls back onto the restaurant floor.

My heart skips a beat as I look at him. I can't help but think how close we were to kissing. How his lips felt in that half a second they brushed against mine. I remind myself I am over Matt and I am avoiding him. I turn away brusquely, glad to see a regular customer at one of my tables waving me down. I hurry over, keeping my back to Matt. When I finish taking the customer's drink order, I can't help but glance back in the direction I saw Matt and Marco standing as I made my way over to the table. They're gone. I try to tell myself that's a good thing, but the disappointment sits in my stomach like a rock, mocking my thoughts.

The restaurant isn't hugely busy tonight, and we keep having quiet moments where we get a chance to chat for a few seconds. Usually in those moments, Matt and I stand together, making up scenarios for our customers, anything from scenes at their workplace to outlandish ideas about what goes on in their bedrooms. Today, that doesn't happen. It soon becomes clear to me that Matt is avoiding me every bit as much as I am avoiding him.

It confirms my thoughts; he has rejected me. Whether that's because he's married or not, I still don't know, but I tell myself it doesn't matter. The last thing I need is a distraction at work, and workplace relationships have always been off limits for me. I'm not about to start changing my principals just because a hot guy almost threw me a bone on a night when he had nothing better to do.

I'm not going to confront him. Chloe was wrong about me. I can do this. I'll just keep avoiding him. If anything, him avoiding me too, is making it easier to do that. Still though, I find my eyes moving to him every time he's around and not looking in my direction. Every time I see him, I feel my heart skip a beat, my pussy gets wet at the thought of what I would like to do to him. I tell myself it's just lust; nothing more. If I tell myself it enough, I might even start to believe it.

A loud party comes into the restaurant, pulling my attention away from Matt for a second. There's four of them. All men, somewhere in their fifties. And they've clearly had a little bit too much to drink. My heart sinks when they choose to sit in my section. I hang back for a moment, looking for Macro. I spot him and gesture to him discreetly.

He comes over. "What?" he says rudely.

I resist the urge to tell him to go and fuck himself and nod towards the table. "Are you allowing them to eat here? They're clearly drunk and kind of loud and they might disturb the other customers." If I tell him I'm uncomfortable waiting on them, there's no way in hell he won't take the opportunity to make me miserable.

Marco looks around the restaurant, actually taking me seriously, but then he looks back at me and shrugs. "They're regulars. And the other diners aren't. It'll be fine Callie. Just be nice to them. Or is that too much to ask?"

"Of course not," I say, biting back my anger. "I just didn't want to get the blame when they empty the place."

They're talking too loud already, cursing and laughing and I notice an elderly couple sitting at the next table give them a wary glance. I start to make my way over, ready to try and diffuse the situation. I approach the elderly couple. "Are you enjoying your meals?" I ask brightly.

They nod, neither of them really looking at me.

I lean in closer and lower my voice, "I can move you if you'd be more comfortable somewhere a little quieter," I say.

"Thank you," the woman says, finally looking up and meeting my eye. I can see the relief on her face. "It's our anniversary and we just wanted a nice meal in peace."

I nod my understanding and lead the couple to a different table, carrying their plates for them. I go back for the drinks. One of the men from the loud table whistles in my direction. I bristle and ignore him.

"Hey, waitress," he shouts.

I turn around slowly, my face full of thunder. "I'll be with you in a minute," I say through gritted teeth. "And my name isn't waitress."

"Ooh, she's feisty!" One of them laughs, getting a round of cheers from the table.

Fucking great.

I take the old couple their drinks, noting that at least they look more comfortable now. The rest of the diners in my section are a little younger themselves and they just ignore the loud table.

I make my way towards the table, already knowing how this is going to go and dreading it. "Are you ready to order?" I ask, putting on my *more fake than usual* smile. The one I keep for customers just like these.

"How about you to go?" one of them asks.

"How about we stick to the menu," I say to another round of cheers.

They make a show of looking at the menu.

"Does the meatball special come with a side of hot waitress?" the same asshole asks.

"Nope. It comes with a side of garlic bread like it says right there," I say.

"Shame," he replies. "You look like the sort of girl who would appreciate a ride on a more experienced man."

I feel sick at his words. As if I'd go there. I try to ignore the jibes, but I'm getting more and more uncomfortable by the second. I could just walk away, but I'll only have to come back, and no doubt, Marco will get in my face about it. I can feel my face going red, the heat spreading down my neck. This doesn't go unnoticed by the table.

"Aww she's blushing. How cute." He laughs.

"Look... do you want to order an actual meal off the actual menu or not?" I snap.

"Relax." He smiles. "A girl doesn't wear a tight little skirt like that unless she wants some attention."

"It's the staff uniform," I point out, biting back my argument that actually I can wear whatever the fuck I want to and not want his attention.

Before I know what's happening, he reaches out and runs his hand up my thigh.

I slap it away, no longer caring if I piss him off. "Take your hand off me right now," I snarl as I shove it away.

His demeanor changes instantly. Gone is the jovial laughter, the fake charm, replaced with a look of cold anger.

I feel nerves fluttering in my stomach. This is going to get ugly.

"Who the fuck do you think you are? Stuck up little cunt," he snarls at me.

I take an involuntary step backwards, stunned at the venom in his words. I open my mouth although I have no idea what to even say to that. I am dangerously close to tears but I refuse to cry in front of the table of idiots. Before I can gather my composure, I hear Matt's voice from behind me. "What did you just call her?" It's level, low, but I can hear the anger simmering dangerously underneath the surface.

The man at the table snickers. "You heard me."

"Yes. I did," Matt says. "But what I can't for the life of me work out is why you thought it was ok to put your hands on her in the first place, or why you think that kind of language is something we'll tolerate."

"She loves it." He grins, not looking at Matt.

"Get the fuck out of here and don't come back," Matt says to the man.

He looks up, his eyes widening when he sees the intense look on Matt's face.

The tears I was holding back have receded a little and I take a step forward, ready to intervene if things go wrong.

"I'm a paying customer," the man says. "And I know the owner."

"No you don't. You know the manager," Matt says.

He says it with such authority I don't doubt his words, although I wonder how he knows for sure. He must have heard Marco telling me they're good customers and to just get on with waiting on them.

"I won't tell you again. Get out," he adds.

The customer smirks at him.

One of the others at the table stands up, trying to maintain what little dignity the party might have left. "Come on Fred, we don't need this shit from some stuck up waiter. We'll go somewhere else and we won't ever come back here." He directs the last part of his sentence to Matt.

He smiles coldly at him. "See that you don't, because you're no longer welcome here. Any of you."

The man who stood up saunters away followed by the other two. Fred, the mouth of the group stays in his seat.

It's clear from the look on Matt's face, barely concealed rage, that he has had enough of him. He reaches out and grabs two fistfuls of the asshole's shirt and drags him to his feet.

Fred's jaw drops, his eyes widening and there's fear in his face. It's finally occurred to him that Matt isn't messing around and that he isn't going to let this go.

Matt releases Fred's shirt and shoves him backwards. Fred stumbles but keeps his footing. He turns around and makes for the door, Matt following close behind him, making sure he doesn't try to change his mind. The whole way to the door, Fred shouts obscenities which Matt ignores.

The shouting brings Marco back to the floor.

Every customer is watching the scene unfolding before them, the restaurant silent now except for Fred's belligerent cursing, and Marco's face is blazing with thunder as he starts across the dining room. Fred finally reaches the door, which Matt shoves him through and then slams shut behind him. Matt stays in place, watching through the glass panel in the door to make sure Fred and his cronies really are leaving.

"Sorry about that ladies and gentleman," Marco says loudly, a charming smile on his face as he addresses the diners.

It does the trick. They go back to their meals, the scene over, and the hubbub of conversation fills the room once more.

Marco reaches Matt. "A word," he says.

Matt follows Marco across the floor, rolling his eyes.

"You too," Marco says to me.

I follow behind him dutifully. Matt brushes my arm with his hand. I look up, telling myself to keep my cool.

"*Are you okay?*" Matt mouths.

I nod, my cool gone as I look into his eyes and see the concern there. I don't know how he can give me one look and completely change the way I feel about him, but he seems to do it effortlessly.

Marco leads us through to the back of the restaurant. The instant we're out of earshot of the diners, he rounds on us. "What the fucking hell just happened?" he demands.

"That fucking dick thought it was acceptable to touch one of the waitresses. And when she rightfully told him not to touch her, he called her a cunt. So I told him to leave and not bother coming back. That's what you would have done. Right?" Matt says, his voice challenging Marco to argue the point.

Marco looks away from Matt with a roll of his eyes. He turns his attention on me. "Where did he touch you?" he asks.

"Here," I say, pointing to my upper thigh. "He was moving his hand higher too until I pushed him away."

Marco rolls his eyes again. "So he wasn't groping your pussy or anything? Honestly Callie, you're so damned sensitive. Part of your job is entertaining customers and not taking offence at every damned thing. I don't know why you think you're too good for this job, but let me tell you something. You're not."

I am shocked by his words. This is a new low, even for Marco. "You're kidding me right? My job is to wait on customers and make sure their dining experience with us is a good one. It is most certainly not in my job description to be a whore," I say.

"Stop being so dramatic. I wasn't suggesting you should become a whore. Just learn to take a joke. Those men are some of our best paying customers."

"Were," Matt puts in.

"Were what?" Marco frowns.

"Were some of your best paying customers. They are banned from the restaurant now."

"Who the hell do you think you are?" Marco demands. "I'm the manager in this branch not you, and I'll say who is banned and who isn't."

Matt takes a step closer to Marco. "He touched one of your staff and you did nothing about it. Whose side do you think head office will take?"

Marco's face changes. He knows he's gone too far, and in the back of his mind, he knows he would have agreed with Matt if it was any other waitress that this had happened to. He makes one last ditch attempt to dig himself out of the hole he's gotten himself into. "We only have Callie's word for that and she has a habit of exaggerating," Marco says.

Matt lunges for him. I grab his arm just in time and I position myself between the two men. Matt's face is full of thunder as he looks over the top of me to Marco. He takes another step forward and I put my hands on his taut chest. I know I can't physically stop him from going after Marco, but I also know he won't hurt me so if I just stay between them, I think I can diffuse this situation. At least I hope I can.

I keep my eyes on Matt as I speak to Marco, "Marco I think you misunderstood, but now you get it. Matt did the right thing and those perverts are banned from the restaurant." I risk a glance over my shoulder. Marco has retreated several paces and I can see the fear on his face as Matt keeps his piercing glare on him.

"Yes. That's right," Marco says, his voice barely audible.

"Good," I say. "Now if you don't mind, can you cover our sections for a moment. Matt and I are going to go and take our breaks."

Marco skulks away.

Matt makes to go after him, but I stand my ground and he backs down. "He's not worth it Matt," I say.

"I know. But you are and I won't have him or anyone else treating you like shit," he says.

I feel a rush of warmth run through me at his words and I smile warmly at him. "Thank you. I'm grateful for what you did with those customers. That was getting out of hand and I didn't know how to rein it back in again. But trust me, I can handle Marco."

Matt relaxes a little bit.

I move my hands reluctantly from his chest. "Come on. Let's go outside and get a breath of fresh air."

Matt nods and we walk along the hallway. Matt props the fire exit open and we step out into the cool evening. I lean my back against the wall and Matt stands facing me. I am suddenly nervous like I don't know what to say to him anymore.

"Listen Callie, about Friday..." Matt starts.

"It's fine. You don't need to explain. I know what happened," I interrupt him.

He frowns and then smiles. "Enlighten me then. What do you think happened?"

"You got caught up in the moment and went to kiss me, and then your wife called and you remembered yourself," I say with a shrug. I was determined not to confront him, but I can't bear to listen to some lame apology and another lie.

"Wife? What wife?" Matt asks.

He sounds so genuinely confused that I dare to believe I have gotten this wrong. "You're telling me you're single?" I say, trying to keep the hope out of my voice.

"That's exactly what I'm telling you." He moves closer to me and he stands with one hand at either side of my shoulders on the wall.

He is close enough to me that I can smell him, sweet cologne and a spicy, more exotic smell beneath it, and the scent of him and his closeness to me makes my pussy clench.

He looks at me, fire burning in his eyes. "I know I don't talk about myself much Callie, but know this about me. I am no cheat. When I'm with a woman, she is mine and only mine. And I am hers and only hers."

His words send a thrill through my body. The intensity of his gaze holds mine and I lose myself in his eyes, his words running through my body like flames. "So what did happen then?" I ask in a quiet voice.

"I'm not worried about what did happen. I'm more concerned with what didn't." He leans in closer to me, and this time, his lips don't just brush mine, they mash against them.

He takes me by surprise and I gasp beneath his kiss. I feel him go to pull away, taking my gasp as a sign I don't want him to kiss me. I wrap my arms around his waist, pulling him against me, not ready to let him go again.

He slips his hands beneath my shoulders, moving me from the wall and wrapping his arms around me. I can feel his strong arms holding me, his chest against mine. I can feel his cock pressed against my crotch, hard and eager for me.

My pussy tingles as his tongue pushes my lips apart, probing into my mouth, claiming it as his. I relax into the kiss, tasting Matt's tongue as he kisses me like he's been unleashed. My hands roam up and down his back, pulling his body even tighter against mine. He pushes one hand into my hair, the other one moving down my back and coming to rest on my waist.

He moans into my mouth as I move my hips slightly, creating friction on his already hard cock. My insides are a boiling mess of desire as our kiss deepens, becoming almost desperate in its intensity.

We jump apart just in time as a coughing sound comes from the hallway. I quickly run my hands through my hair as Matt grins at me, a grin so full of lust and need that it makes my clit pulse.

James appears in the doorway. "Hey. Marco sent me to make sure you two are okay," he says.

More like he sent him to make sure we haven't just walked out after what happened. He didn't even have the balls to come and check on us himself. "Everything's fine," I say. "We're coming back in now."

"Cool," James says. "Why wouldn't things be okay? Don't tell me he was pissed that you threw those losers out."

"He was at first, then he heard what happened before he appeared," Matt explains while leaving out the main chunk of the story.

"Ah, makes sense," James says then turns and heads back inside.

I go to follow him. Matt catches my hand and I turn to him.

"This isn't over," he says quietly enough that only I can hear him. His voice is full of lust, his eyes meeting mine and sending fire through me once more. "I intend to finish what I started." He releases my hand.

I hurry inside. As I go back towards the dining room, I slide my phone out of my apron pocket and send a quick text message to Chloe.

"I owe you a beer."

Chapter Nine

MATT

I was determined to stay away from Callie. I can't allow myself to become distracted from the real reason I'm here, especially not now as I get closer to the truth. But it's easier said than done when it comes to her.

I've spent most of my shift trying my best to avoid her, but everywhere I went, I could hear her laughing, or smell her perfume as I walked through a space she had just been in. It didn't help my resolve any that several times I caught her watching me when she thought I wasn't looking.

The final straw came when that fucking pervert put his hand on her and then had the downright gall to call her a cunt. What sort of a man talks to a woman that way? I think I know the answer to that one, but no one talks to her that way. No one.

It felt good throwing him out, showing him that he has no power here. And Marco won't be a problem, I've seen to that.

I was shocked to discover Callie thought I was married, although I guess in some ways it makes sense that she might think that after my hasty retreat on Friday from the party. That wasn't because of Callie though. It just had to be done.

When we finally kissed outside of the restaurant, it was everything I had dreamed it would be and more. I could taste her hunger for me, and it took everything I had not to fuck her right then and there against that wall. I was so annoyed when James interrupted us, although now, I think maybe it was a good thing. That's not how I want my first time with Callie to be, up against a wall in some sordid little alley way.

I was serious about this not being over though. I know it shouldn't happen, but I also know it's going to. I'm done fighting this. I'm going to make love to Callie so hard. I'm going to make her come over and over again, until I know she is well and truly mine.

And I will just have to hope when the truth comes out and the dust settles, she can forgive me for lying about who I am and why I'm here.

Chapter Ten

CALLIE

I spend the rest of my shift on cloud nine. I keep remembering the feel of Matt's lips on mine. I keep seeing the way he looked at me when he told me in no uncertain terms he's no cheater. Most of all, I keep hearing him tell me this isn't over. Goosebumps break out over my whole body every time I think of him saying that to me, every time I picture the look on his face when he said it.

There's still so much I don't know about Matt. I still don't know what happened on Friday. Who it was that called him or what was so important that he couldn't wait five minutes to tell me why he had to leave. And I still don't know why he has been missing from work for most of the week. Maybe I'll ask him. Maybe I won't. Right now, all I care about is that he isn't married. That and the fact he seems to want me like I want him. That's all that matters really.

Marco has finished work for the night, which has definitely helped my mood too. He hasn't said anything else to me, in fact, he's avoided me altogether. I'm pleased about that, but I have a feeling this whole thing won't be over just yet. Marco will find a way to have a go at me when Matt isn't around. But like I told Matt, I can handle Marco. His being a prick to me is nothing new.

Sasha comes over to me, her coat on and her handbag slung over her shoulder. "I'm done." She grins. "Don't tell Marco I went out the front way, he'd have a fit."

"I won't," I promise her.

There is just one table finishing up the last of their desserts and then we'll be closing for the night. Sasha is the last one to leave the restaurant except for Matt and I who are on the locking up shift together. We've managed to get all of the cleaning up done already. All that's left to do is wipe down the table that's in use and mop the floor.

The couple on the remaining table seem to be done, and I try my best not to hover or make it clear to them that we're closed. Luckily, they don't need the hint. The man waves at me and asks for the bill which I gladly bring him. He leaves cash on the table, enough to cover the bill and a cracking tip. On the way out, he apologizes for overstaying his welcome. I tell him he hasn't and wish him a good night. With a tip like that, an extra ten minutes on the end of my shift is easily worth it.

I lock the door behind the couple and ring their bill through the register, pocketing my tip. I quickly wipe their table over and then run the mop over the floor. There's no sign of Matt through any of this and I wonder where he's gotten too. As much as I complained to Chloe about Matt slacking off, I can see now she was right about her theory of that as well as being right about the fact that I should confront Matt. I was angry with him for rejecting me. He doesn't usually slack off.

I finish up the floor, dump out the water and return the mop and bucket to the cleaning cupboard. I go to the staff room. I take my tips from my apron pocket and put them in my handbag and then I hang my apron up and collect my things. I expected to find Matt in the staff room, but it's empty. I frown to myself and check the back door. It's locked so Matt has been here. I flick the light off and leave the room.

I decide he must be in the bathroom and I head back towards the dining room to wait for him. It's not like he could have left without saying goodbye. I gave him my keys earlier to lock up the back shutter, and he hasn't returned them, so he's here somewhere.

As I pass Marco's office, I notice the light is on. I roll my eyes. If we leave any lights on, we catch a shit load of trouble for wasting company resources, but apparently, it's okay for Marco to go home and leave his lights on. It's not worth bringing it up with him. He'll find a way to turn it around and make it my fault no doubt.

I push the door open, planning on turning the light off. I stop in my tracks when I see Matt sitting behind Marco's desk, his feet resting on the desk, his hands crossed behind his head.

"What are you doing?" I ask.

He grins as he gets up and crosses the room to stand before me. "Waiting for you. I was starting to think you would never show up." He doesn't give me a chance to respond. Instead, he grabs me by the hand and pulls me against him. He drops my hand and wraps his arms around me, pressing his lips against mine.

I am taken aback and for a second, I don't respond, but then I feel the stirring low down in my stomach, the throbbing in my clit, and I kiss Matt back. My arms go around him, pulling him tightly against me as his tongue snakes into my mouth. My hands move up and down his back, and before I can stop myself, I am pulling his shirt out of his trousers. I slide my hands beneath it, running my palms over the bare skin of his back. I trail my nails over his skin as he moves his lips from mine, kissing down my neck. I put my head back, exposing my throat and he runs his tongue up the center of it, sending shivers through my body.

He moves back up to my mouth and our lips meet again. His kiss starts off slow and tender, the kind of kiss that makes me feel warm inside. It soon intensifies as his desire bubbles inside of him, spurring him on. The warmth inside of me heats up, becoming a burning fire that consumes me.

He pulls back from my lips and we look at each other, our breaths coming in pants. I want him so badly. He reaches out and takes hold of my hips. He turns me and pulls me towards him, my back against his chest. He begins to slowly unbutton my shirt. As he opens my buttons, he whispers in my ear, "I told you I was going to finish what I started didn't I? I can't wait another minute for this Callie."

That makes two of us then. His breath tickles my skin and sends a wild rush of goosebumps over my skin. I reach behind me and rub my hand over the bulge in his trousers, feeling his hard cock. He nibbles my neck as he opens my last button. He spins me again, pulling my hand away from his cock. He pushes the shirt down my arms and it falls to the ground. I reach behind myself and unhook my bra, throwing it to the ground with my shirt.

Matt makes an appreciative noise in the back of his throat and I feel my pussy flood with desire when it hits me that this gorgeous man is as enchanted by me as I am by him. I step forward and run my hand over the front of his trousers again.

He cups my face with his hands and kisses me. He walks me backwards as he does, leading me to the couch in the corner of the office.

I didn't think we'd go all of the way here, but as my knees hit the couch and I tumble backwards onto it, I know we will. And I know I won't try to stop this from happening. The fact it's taboo to have sex here only turns me on more.

Matt doesn't immediately follow me onto the couch. Instead, he stands before me. I can see his chest rising and falling as he attempts to control his breathing. I reach out and push my hands beneath his shirt, running them over his rock hard abs and up to his chest. I go to stand back up, but Matt puts his hands on my shoulders, holding me in place. I look up at him questioningly and he smiles down at me.

He gets to his knees and takes hold of my calves, pulling them forward. My ass scoots along the couch and I find myself perched precariously on the edge of it. Matt reaches behind me and opens the button on my skirt and then the zipper.

I lift my ass as he hooks his fingers into the waistband, letting him slide it down my legs and off me. I lift my ass again and he comes back for my panties. I feel suddenly self-conscious being naked in front of him when he is fully clothed and I reach for the top button of his shirt. I unbutton it and move onto the next one. The whole time I open his buttons, Matt keeps his eyes locked on mine. By the time I have his shirt open and off, I am squirming with need, my pussy wetter than I've ever felt it. A shiver goes through me. If he can do that to me with just a look, what can he do to me with his fingers, his tongue, his cock?

I don't have to wait long to find out. Matt stays in position for a couple of seconds as I run my hands over his body. I manage to tear my eyes away from his long enough to run them over his body. His skin is lightly tanned, his muscles tight and ripped. I make a groaning sound of longing as I drink him in.

He touches my shoulders again, pushing me backwards and I feel the back of the couch against my upper back. Matt runs his hands up my calves, tickling the skin there with his light touch. When he reaches my knees, he grabs them, roughly pulling my legs apart. He leans forwards, his face only inches from my pussy. He takes a deep breath, inhaling my scent, and he lets it out in a low moan that sends a throbbing through my clit.

He moves closer and just when I think I can't take it any longer, can't wait another second, his tongue finds my clit. I am instantly aware of the throbbing of it as his hungry mouth clamps down swallowing my engorged nub and sucking almost frenziedly but with a magical action. I gasp, his skill sending shocks of pleasure through my stomach. No man has ever done that to me and I love it. He puts his hands beneath my knees, lifting my legs and depositing them on his shoulders. He runs his hands along my thighs, resting them on the tops of them. He takes hold of my swollen clit between his lips and moves his tongue over my nub faster and faster and I can feel my climax building as he works me intensely. I squeeze my thighs together, pushing his face tighter against me, forcing him to apply even more pressure to my clit. He moves one of his hands from my thigh and I feel his fingers pushing into my slick pussy. I moan as he penetrates me, his fingers working beautifully claiming my pussy as his tongue claims my clit.

The sensation makes my pussy clench around his fingers while his tongue works magic. My climax is almost upon me now. My breathing is a series of ragged pants as he pushes me closer and closer to the edge. He speeds his fingers up and just as I am about to crash into my orgasm, he expertly sucks my clit into his mouth.

I arch my back, an ahh sound coming from me as my fists bunch at my sides. He sucks on my clit again and my orgasm washes over me, a tingling heat that starts in my clit and moves through my stomach, making my muscles contract. He slips his fingers out of my clenching pussy and moves his tongue through my slit. He puts his mouth against my opening and sucks, drinking in the juices that pour from me as my orgasm intensifies.

His probing fingers find my clit and press down on it. I feel the tendons in my neck stretching as my body goes rigid. My breath leaves me in a rush and I try to gasp in another one, but for a moment, I am paralyzed held in place by the plea-sure coursing through my body. Finally, his rubbing fingers slow their pace and I suck in a ragged breath that burns my throat. He chooses that moment to push his tongue inside my pussy and my orgasm hits its peak, lighting up every cell in my body. My breath blasts out of me, his name on my lips, a scream so full of primal lust that it sounds more animal than human.

Matt sits back on his heels, looking at my pussy in lust. I take the few seconds he's distracted to get my breath back a little bit. Seeing him like this, his cheeks flushed, his hair mussed up, his eyes shining with lust and my juices coating the bottom half of his face sends a rush of need through me.

I sit back up, reaching for him. He leans closer and kisses me. The salty taste of my juices mingling with the sweet taste of

Matt's mouth almost sends me over the edge again. I shuffle closer to Matt, wrapping my legs around his waist and pulling him against me as I kiss him hungrily.

His hands move up and down my back, his fingers leaving trails of fire where they touch. He wraps his arms around me tightly and gets to his feet, lifting me with him. He keeps one hand on my waist, the other he moves beneath my body and opens his trousers. He pushes them to the floor and steps out of them. His boxers follow. He runs his fingers through my slit, rubbing my juices over me, leaving me slick and ready for him.

He grabs his cock and lines it up with my opening. He's fucking huge. Long and so thick. He knows there's no need for any lubrication and slams it into me with one hard thrust and I gasp as he fills me, stretches me. He's deep inside, our skins merging as he gives me every inch of that beautiful cock. He kisses down my neck as his hips begin to move. "You are mine now Callie," he says in a low, husky voice.

I cling to him, moving my hips in time with his, riding his huge cock, feeling it moving deep inside of me, marking its territory and claiming my pussy. I feel my head fall back, my hair tickling my back. Matt is wild as he runs his tongue down my throat and across my chest. He excitedly sucks one of my nipples into his mouth, flicking his tongue over it as he suckles. He grips it gently in his teeth and the bouncing motion of our thrusts makes it tug slightly, sending a wave of perfect pain through me.

He tightens his hold on it and I gasp, loving the feeling of the stinging pain mixing with the pleasure that's filling my body. I lift my head back up as he releases my nipple and our mouths slam together again.

I push my hands into his hair, tugging it as I feel my orgasm starting to build again. Matt gasps in a breath as I tug and our kiss is broken. We look into each other's eyes for a moment and then Matt is moving, walking me back to the couch. He stays inside of me as he lays me down on my back and gets on top of me. He pulls his hips back and slams his cock into me, going deeper than before, making me gasp again as a delicious stinging feeling throbs through my pussy and into my stomach.

I meet his thrust with desperate thrusts of my own, slamming myself onto his cock. I run my nails down his bare back, digging them in slightly as he thrusts faster and faster. My orgasm hits me without warning, exploding through my body, pinning me to the couch as every nerve ending in my body turns to fire. My body pulses with ecstasy as Matt continues to pound into me. I press my face against his neck, whispering his name over and over again as the pleasure consumes me and whisks me away.

I feel my pussy clench around his cock, and as it clenches, Matt moans my name. His cock throbs inside of me and I feel a rush of warmth as he comes in me. I clench around him again, on purpose this time, squeezing his cock, milking every drop of cum from him.

He moans my name again, and then we are still. He rests his head on my shoulder and I wrap my arms around him as we lay still for a moment, getting our breaths back.

Just as I start to feel like I am in control of myself again, Matt lifts his head from my shoulder. He brushes his lips against mine and then smiles down at me. "Was I worth waiting for?" he asks.

I make a *hmm* sound and scrunch my face up as though I'm thinking.

Matt laughs and shakes his head. He gets up, reaches down and helps me up.

I begin to get dressed, watching as Matt does the same.

"Enjoying the view?" Matt asks with a raised eyebrow.

"Yeah," I say. "And yeah, you were worth waiting for."

He crosses to my side to pull me into his arms and kisses me again.

I laugh and wriggle away after a couple of minutes. "Stop it! Or we'll still be here when the cleaners get here."

Reluctantly, he lets me go and I finish getting dressed. I excuse myself to go to the bathroom. As I pee, I can't stop myself from grinning. Sex with Matt was everything I had hoped it would be and a lot more. I have never come like that before, not even once, and Matt made it happen twice.

I finish up and go to the mirror. I run my fingers through my hair, trying to tease it back into some sort of order. I smile to myself when I see my flushed cheeks and my swollen red lips, a reminder of Matt's lips on mine.

Chapter Eleven

MATT

I watch Callie's ass as she walks away from me to go to the bathroom. I don't mean to, I just can't help myself. She's so fucking sexy I can't stop myself from looking at her every chance I get.

As she leaves the room, I sigh contentedly and finish buttoning my shirt back up. I can't believe it's finally happened. After what feels like forever trying to resist Callie, I've finally claimed her. She's mine now.

My cock stirs at the thought and I try to think of something other than Callie's tight little pussy, something other than how fucking sweet she tasted. Like I can think of anything else after that. I'm tempted to follow her to the bathroom and fuck her against the sinks, but I resist the urge. I really don't want the cleaning staff to come in and catch us fucking in the bathroom like teenagers.

Instead, I take a last look at the couch, unable to wipe the grin from my face. I grab Callie's handbag and jacket, flick the lights off then leave the office. I wait in the hallway.

She doesn't keep me waiting long. She smiles when she sees me holding her handbag. "It suits you."

"Really? I always thought purple was more my color," I joke as I hand her things to her.

She laughs as she puts her jacket on and hooks her handbag over her shoulder. "Ready?"

No. I won't ever be ready to not have you by my side. "Yup," I say aloud.

We lock up the restaurant and Callie glances at her watch. "Dammit. We missed the last train," she says.

"Yeah I know. Don't worry. I'll call a cab. I can drop you off on the way," I tell her.

She opens her mouth to argue, but then she thinks better of it and nods her head. It's not like I'm going to let her walk home and she knows it.

"Hungry?" I ask her.

"Yeah, I'm starving."

"Good. There's a twenty-four hour diner just down the road. We can grab a quick bite and then head home if you like," I say.

She nods and I hold my arm out to her. She slips her hand through it and we begin to walk.

"Aren't you meant to buy me dinner before you fuck me?" she asks.

I snort out a laugh, her words taking me by surprise. "Traditionally yes, but something tells me you're not into the traditional stuff. That you prefer to make your own rules."

"And break them it seems." She grins.

"Break them?" I ask.

She nods. "I always said I would never get involved with a colleague and yet, here we are."

"In your defense, you didn't know someone like me was going to come and work with you though did you?"

"Modest aren't you?" She laughs.

We reach the diner and I hold the door open for her, watching her ass again as she slips through. "I do try to be," I say.

Callie shakes her head but she laughs. I lead her to a booth in the almost deserted diner and we sit down. She picks up the menu and I follow suit, even though I already know what I'm ordering. I watch Callie as her eyes scan the menu. Her tongue pokes out the corner of her mouth as she reads. As I watch her, I feel a warm feeling in my stomach.

Callie puts the menu down.

"You know what you want?" I ask her.

"Cheeseburger and fries," she says. "You can't come to a place like this and not get that can you?"

"And a chocolate milkshake," we both say together and laugh.

I go up to the counter and place our order and pay for the food. I go back to the booth and Callie and I sit in companionable silence waiting for our food. Her stomach growls and we both laugh.

"I told you I was starving," she says.

We don't have to wait too long before our meals arrive and we dive in. Callie dips fries in ketchup and nibbles on them, chewing slowly, almost thoughtfully.

"What are you thinking about?" I ask her. I curse myself for the lame line.

Callie doesn't seem to notice. Instead, she just shakes her head and laughs. "Honestly. I was just thinking how much I'm dreading work tomorrow. I'm on the lunch time shift and we're always short staffed for the lunch crowd. And well, I guess I was thinking that it will be weird for us not doing the same shift tomorrow. I kind of like closing up with you and getting the train home together."

"So have dinner with me tomorrow night," I blurt out. It's not a spur of the moment thing. I knew the second I kissed Callie earlier today I was going to take her to dinner tomorrow night, but I had planned on asking her a much better way.

"You're meant to be on the closing shift at the restaurant," she says.

"I'll get out of it." I shrug. "I'll make something up." I won't make anything up. I'll just tell Marco I won't be in. It's not like he can fire me for missing a shift.

"Okay..." Callie smiles. "It's a date." She blushes furiously as she realizes what she's just said. "I mean—"

"It is a date," I cut her off. I know I'm doing what I swore I wouldn't do. I'm letting Callie get under my skin, letting her distract me from what I'm meant to be doing. But she's worth it. I'll find a way to still do what I have to do and get the girl.

She smiles at me, a warm, happy smile that makes my heart skip a beat. I want to tell her the truth, tell her everything. But I can't. Not yet. I just have to hope that when I do, she can find it in her heart to forgive me for not telling her sooner.

Chapter Twelve

CALLIE

"*I* knew you wouldn't be able to hold out on confronting Matt." Chloe laughs. She takes a long drink of her beer and holds it in the air to sigh dramatically. "Ahhh, the sweet taste of victory."

"Okay, okay, you got me!" I laugh. "But I did last a good few hours."

"Yeah, but you spent those hours avoiding him Callie. How long did you last after speaking to him?"

"About four minutes." I cringe.

Chloe laughs and shakes her head. "Look it all worked out for the best, didn't it? He's not married, and he's clearly into you. Why can't you just relax and enjoy it?"

Why can't I? Last night couldn't have gone better. Matt isn't married, we'd had the best sex of my life and I will be going on a date with him tonight after a quick drink with Chloe. What more could I possibly ask for? "It's just... I don't know. I can't put my finger on it. But I feel like he's hiding something from me. Something big. He told me he wasn't married and I believe him, but he still didn't tell me who was on the phone that night."

"Maybe he thinks he doesn't have to explain himself to someone he hasn't even been on a date with yet," Chloe suggests, somewhat unhelpfully.

"Gee thanks for that Captain Obvious." I laugh.

"All I'm saying is give him a chance. You haven't told him about the skeletons in your closet, so why do you expect him to tell you every detail of his life?"

"I don't have skeletons in my closet," I point out.

"Really? So Matt knows Marco is a dick to you because you turned him down, does he?"

"Well no, but that's hardly a skeleton is it? I haven't told Matt because there's nothing to tell, and I really don't want to even think about Marco when I'm with Matt."

"Exactly. And maybe he has something similar that's not really going to affect your relationship, but it's just messy and something he doesn't feel the need to tell you."

"Maybe," I relent.

Truth be told, I kind of tuned out after Chloe said the word relationship. Are Matt and I in a relationship? It's too soon to think that way. We had one great night, but that doesn't mean anything does it? I don't want to get ahead of myself and come across as some psycho that starts signing my name as *Mrs Callie... Mrs Callie who?* It occurs to me suddenly that I don't even know Matt's last name.

"Where's he taking you anyway?" Chloe asks, interrupting my thoughts.

"I'm not sure... I just know we're going for dinner, and he's picking me up at seven."

"Seven?" Chloe says. "You realize it's six thirty now right?"

"What? No. Shit," I curse, checking my watch and seeing she's right. I planned on going home to get changed, but that's out of the window now. It'll take me until after seven to get back to my dorm room. I look down at my outfit. A pink dress that sits on my mid-thigh. It's cute, but it's not really restaurant cute. I shrug. It'll have to do. "I'll text him for the address of the place."

I type out a quick text to Matt explaining that I'm running a little late and ask for the address of the restaurant so I can meet him there. My phone rings almost the instant I send the message.

It's Matt.

"I won't be a minute," I say to Chloe, hurrying out of the bar and into the street. I take Matt's call. "Hello?"

"Hey. Where are you? I'll swing by and get you," he says.

I consider it, but the last thing I need is Chloe blurting out something embarrassing to Matt. "It's fine. I'll just catch a cab." I hope the place isn't too far away. I could really do without wasting my money on a cab.

"Well, if you're sure..." Matt says.

I tell him I'm sure, and he gives me the address. I go back into the bar and ask Chloe if she's heard of the street.

She nods. "It's not far from here actually. It's only a five minute walk. Just go to the end of the block, turn right and keep going. What's the place called?"

"The Herb Garden," I say.

Chloe lets out a low whistle.

"What?"

"Well, let's just say that if you had any doubts as to whether or not Matt's really into you, you can let them go. That place is fucking expensive. Like millionaire expensive. If he's taking you there on a waiter's salary, he probably won't be able to eat for the rest of the month."

The thought should cheer me up. I should be happy to know Matt is that into me, but it doesn't. I don't like the idea of him spending half of his salary on trying to impress me. I would have been happy to go back to the diner we went to last night.

"Honestly Callie, the guy can't do anything right in your eyes can he?" Chloe says, reading my expression.

"I just don't like the thought of him spending so much money on me. It's not like I can return the favor is it?"

"Just make sure you give him a b j he never forgets." Chloe winks.

"Thanks, that's helpful." I laugh then pick my drink up and down the rest. "I best get going."

"I'll walk to the end of the street with you," Chloe says.

We leave the bar. The fresh air coupled with the beer starts to take effect and I feel myself relaxing a little bit. I decide to just enjoy the night and see where it goes. If we decide on another date, then I'll talk to Matt and tell him not to blow his budget this way again.

We reach the end of the block and Chloe and I part ways. I walk along the street, checking the names of the places as I go. I pass a few restaurants dotted amongst them are boutique shops closed for the night. A couple of the shops remain open. This is a part of town I rarely come to and it definitely seems like it's getting more high-end the further along the street I walk. I pass a cocktail bar and another restaurant. Finally, I spot The Herb Garden. My stomach does a flip when I see Matt standing casually outside waiting for me.

He's wearing a suit, an actual fucking suit. And I'm dressed like we're going for a picnic in the park. This is seriously bad. I honestly think I would have turned and fled if it wasn't for the fact that Matt has clearly spotted me.

He doesn't look pleased to see me. He frowns when he sees me and quickly comes towards me, closing the gap between us.

"What's wrong?" I ask.

I already know the answer. He's annoyed because I'm so underdressed.

"You said you were getting a cab," he says, his voice sounding like he's barely holding back his temper.

His words throw me. What the fuck? Why is he checking up on me? "I was only around the corner. I didn't recognize the name of the street, but Chloe told me where it was. Since when did you start checking up on my movements?"

He relaxes a little and sighs. "I'm not checking up on you. I just don't like the idea of you wandering around the streets alone like this," he says.

My heart warms at his concern, my annoyance at him for checking up on me fades, and I smile. "Because you're an international spy and you're worried your arch enemy will kidnap me to teach you a lesson?" I tease him.

"Yes. Exactly that." He leans in and kisses my cheek.

I get a whiff of his aftershave. His lips are warm on my skin and I instantly feel tingles going through me.

"Seriously though, I would have picked you up," he says.

"It's fine, I'm here now."

"Yes, you are, and you look amazing by the way." He smiles.

He holds his arm out but I don't take it. He frowns at me. "What is it?"

"I don't look amazing. I look like what I am – like I've come straight from college. I'm not dressed for this kind of place Matt."

"Not true. You'd look amazing no matter what you're wearing," he insists.

I can't help but smile. "Look I get that you're being nice, but seriously, you're all suited up and look at me. I probably won't even get through the door." I am most definitely regretting the flat sandals as well as the dress now.

"I know the owner. You'll be fine," he says with a laugh.

I'm not convinced.

Matt looks at me for a minute and then he grins. "Wait here a minute."

"Why? Where are you going?" I ask.

He kisses my cheek again and squeezes my hand. "Just wait here." He's gone without another word.

I watch him walk through a crowd of people who stand outside of a bar laughing. I lose sight of him in the small crowd. I try to spot him again, but I can't. I sigh. What the hell is he doing? I feel self-conscious just standing here like this and I move back to lean against the wall between the restaurant and the shop next door. I pull my phone out and pretend I'm doing something on it. I scroll aimlessly through my Instagram feed, trying to look busy. I keep looking for Matt, but he's nowhere to be seen.

Five minutes pass and then ten. I'm starting to think Matt has mysteriously vanished again. I debate texting him but that would look too desperate. Finally, he reappears again. My jaw drops when I see him.

His suit is gone and he stands before me in jeans, a white t-shirt and a pair of grey sneakers. "There. You feel better now?" He grins as he comes back to my side.

"I — yes." I laugh. "Where the hell did you get those from?"

"The store down the road." He grins.

I shake my head, surprised by his gesture, but much more comfortable in what I'm wearing now. When he offers me his arm again, this time, I take it. "At least now, we'll both get turned away." I chuckle.

He laughs with me, shaking his head. We approach the restaurant.

The doormen greet Matt by his name and ushers us inside. The maître d' also greets Matt by name and I start to relax. He wasn't kidding. He really does know the owner. The maître d' shows us to a table by the window.

Matt thanks him and takes my hand across the table. "Are you okay? If you're really uncomfortable, we can go somewhere else."

"I'm just worried about how expensive it is here," I blurt out.

Matt laughs. "I told you, I know the owner. I get friend rates." He looks around to make sure we're not being over heard and then he leans in closer. "Order whatever you like and I only get charged for the appetizer. Seriously."

I grin at him, starting to relax now. How expensive can an appetizer be? I begin to look over the menu. Everything sounds so delicious. I've barely even glanced at it when a waiter appears.

"Good evening. I have a delicate and delightful Sauvignon Blanc tonight sir, or of course I am happy to recommend a pairing with your dishes," he says.

I force myself to remain causal, like I go to this kind of place all the time. But holy shit. He's no waiter. He's a sommelier. Even our restaurant doesn't have a specific wine guy and we're pretty high end.

Matt chats with him for a moment about the options then he turns to me. "Do you have any preference Callie?"

I shake my head, completely out of my depth. "I'm happy to go with whatever you choose."

Matt orders the Sauvignon Blanc.

When the sommelier walks away, I smile at Matt. "I am so out of my depth here. I would have ordered a glass of rose or something." I laugh.

"Don't worry about it." Matt shrugs. "They rely on people being flummoxed by the options. The sommelier is there to upsell the expensive stuff to people who panic and take his recommendation that's all."

"Like you did?" I grin.

"Yeah, exactly. I mean go big or go home right?"

"Right!" I laugh. I go back to the menu and finally settle on the chicken and tarragon soup, lightly braised beef with seasonal vegetables for my main, and for dessert, chocolate lava cake.

Matt catches a waiter's eye and gives him our order. He orders the duck pâté followed by a rib eye steak with mushrooms and a strawberry cheesecake for dessert.

Before we can really start to chat, the sommelier returns to our table. He opens the wine with a flourish and pours a taster glass out. Matt swirls the wine, studies it for a moment and then sniffs it. He nods his approval and tastes the wine. "Perfect," he says.

The sommelier pours us each a glass and subtly moves away.

I'm beginning to wonder if we'll ever get any peace when an older couple approaches our table. Matt frowns slightly but it doesn't put them off. They hover over our table.

"I thought it was you," the man says, sounding excited. "Let me buy you a drink. What are you having?"

"I'm fine thank you," Matt says. He smiles at the man but it's clearly a fake smile.

"I insist. I've been meaning to call you actually, and —"

"Look this really isn't a good time," Matt says, interrupting the man. He digs in his pocket and pulls out a card which he hands to the man. "Give me a call during business hours and we'll talk."

The man seems to notice me for the first time, and it suddenly clicks for him that Matt and I are on a date. He goes pink and begins to stammer out an apology.

"Really, it's fine," Matt says.

The man's wife finally drags him away from us.

"What the hell was that?" I ask. "Who was he?"

"Give me two minutes," Matt says, standing up. "I'm going to ask to be moved somewhere a little more private."

I'm quite happy here, but I have to admit the idea of being somewhere more private with Matt appeals to me. I want to have him all to myself tonight and not have to keep fending off apparent members of his fan club.

I sip my wine too quickly while I wait for Matt to return. When he comes back with the maître d' who leads us away from the table, I realize I am a little tipsy. The maître d' takes us through an archway to a quiet dining room with only one other couple seated in it. He leads us to the table furthest away from them and apologizes before leaving us alone.

"This is better isn't it?" Matt says.

I nod. It feels more intimate and I like the feeling that we're almost alone here. "Who was the man at the table?" I ask again.

"I have no idea," he says. "Maybe he had me mistaken for someone else."

This doesn't ring true at all. If he had mistaken him for someone else, then why would Matt have given him a card and told him to call him. Why does a damned waiter even have business cards to hand out? "You expect me to believe that?" I demand.

Matt shrugs. "I don't know what else to tell you Callie. I don't know who he was, let alone what was going through his head."

"Okay," I say. "Forget about him. I don't know anything about you."

"You know plenty about me," Matt defends.

He looks uncomfortable, but right now, I don't care. I'm getting sick of all of the secrets. I always thought a man of mystery would be hot, but now, I'm finding out it's actually just frustrating. "I don't know anything substantial about you. Tell me something about yourself. Something real. Or we might as well just call this date done now. For god's sake, I don't even know your last name."

The waiter appears at that moment with our starters.

"The pâté?" he says.

"Me," Matt says.

The waiter puts the pâté down in front of him.

"And soup for the lady," he adds as he sets my soup down.

It smells delicious and I realize I'm starving. I pick up my spoon and taste it. It's every bit as good as it looks. I am suddenly nervous, afraid to look at Matt. He obviously isn't going to talk. And now I've laid down an ultimatum like that one, what do I do? Leave and save face but regret it? Or stay and have Matt think my words mean nothing?

"Hunter. My last name is Hunter." Matt says.

I do look up then and he smiles. I feel myself returning his smile as he goes on.

"I grew up in Belfast," he says. "I was seven when my family moved here. My parents were never particularly strict, but they insisted on manners. I guess my brothers and I were kind of a handful. I'm the eldest of three. Chance is two years younger than me, and then there's Seb, he's only a year behind Chance My family was pretty traditional. Dad went out to work and mom stayed at home to raise us."

"Wow, your mom must be a saint!" I laugh.

"I'm not sure that's how I would have described her." Matt laughs. "But she was a good mother. She loved us all so much and we all knew it. And it's because of her that I developed a love for food. She loved home cooking. She would make every meal from scratch and she would bake the most amazing cakes. She taught me to cook, she taught me how to pair flavors."

"It's funny, you sound more like you should be a chef than a waiter." I smile.

"Maybe you're right, but I have a love for people too. I like to be social, to work on the ground so to speak. I like seeing people happy." He shrugs looking embarrassed suddenly, like he's given too much of himself away.

"I know what you mean. Some customers make our job a pleasure don't they? But boy, some of them make me feel pretty murderous."

"Oh, yeah. I get that. I should maybe say, I like the nice people."

Our waiter reappears with our main courses.

I thank him and dive straight in.

"How did you get into restaurant work?" Matt asks me.

I'm not sure how much to tell him. It's not something I usually talk about, but then again, Matt has finally opened up to me a little and told me about his family. I guess I owe him the same courtesy. I can't complain about him keeping himself closed off from me, if I do the same to him. "I just kind of fell into it. There was no particular love for the environment. I basically needed a job that paid well enough to fund my degree, and that had flexible hours. I had a choice; waitressing or bartending, and I decided I would have to deal with less drunken idiots in a restaurant than in a bar."

Matt raises an eyebrow. "You pay for your own degree?"

"Yeah... my father left my mom before I was even old enough to remember him. And my mom died when I was eighteen, right before I started applying to universities. Our house was rented and we didn't have money really. Her insurance policy barely covered the funeral and that was it. I was on my own."

"I'm sorry," Matt says.

I shrug. "I miss my mom so much. It was always just the two of us. But I'm not worried about paying my way. She always taught me never to get in debt and never to rely on someone else to keep me. I guess the lesson stuck, because I stick around at the restaurant. Even after..." I trail off as the waiter brings our desserts. I smile at Matt. "This looks amazing!" I line my spoon up with the top of the cake. "Are you ready for the ooey, gooey chocolate?" I grin.

"Ooey gooey?" Matt raises a brow at me.

"Yup," I confirm as I push my spoon into the cake and the sauce spills out. "See?"

"I get it." Matt laughs.

I try the cake and make an *mmm* sound. Without thinking, I scoop some up on my spoon and hold it out to Matt. "You have to try this."

I expect him to take the spoon from me, but he doesn't. Instead, he leans forward and I feed him the cake. He doesn't take his eyes from mine as he does it, and I have a quick flash of those lips somewhere else, doing something else. Matt grins at me as I shift in my seat, well aware of the effect he's having on me.

He offers me a taste of his cheesecake and I accept readily, ready to get my own back. I take the bite of cheesecake, which I have to admit is perfection, and I purposely get a bit of cream on my lip, which I then make a show of licking away. Matt smiles and shakes his head. I smirk at him and go back to my dessert secretly pleased that I can have this effect on him.

"Even after what?" Matt asks suddenly.

"Huh?" I ask back.

"Earlier, you said you stick around at the restaurant. Even after... and then you just kind of stopped."

"Oh yeah. Even after Marco hit on me," I say. I know instantly it was a mistake. Matt's face clouds with anger.

"He did fucking what?" he exclaims.

I reach across the table and run my fingers over his hand. "Relax. It was a long time ago. I made it clear I wasn't interested and he's never tried it again." I leave the rest unsaid. The constant dread that it will happen again. The way he treats me as a result of me turning him down. The way I felt cheap for days afterwards, even though nothing happened.

"So that's why he's such an asshole to you then," Matt says.

I'm surprised he noticed. Part of me always thinks it's all in my head, that Marco is a prick to everyone. "Maybe. Or maybe he's just a bad manager."

Matt still looks angry.

Now, I hate that I've ruined the mood of our date. "Look can we just forget I mentioned this? I really don't want to think about work tonight."

Matt nods slowly and then he smiles at me, a playful smile that sends shivers through me. "So what do you *want* to think about?" he asks.

"Oh, I don't know. Something a little more appealing." I grin.

"How about this?" He moves his chair around the table, moving closer to me, leans forward and kisses me.

I feel sparks fly between us as his lips touch mine. It's a short kiss, much shorter than I would have liked it to be, but I remind myself we're in a public place.

Matt pulls back and smiles at me.

Fucking hell, he's hot. "Yeah. That's much better," I say in a husky voice.

He puts his hand on my thigh and I bite my lip as it moves higher. I pick up my wine glass, needing to do something with my hands as Matt's hand finds my panties. He rubs his fingers over the lace, pressing it against me and making me suck in a sharp breath.

He pushes my panties to one side and rubs his thumb over my clit, sending shocks of pleasure through my body. I take a gulp of the wine and set it back down. My hands move to the edge of the table, gripping it so hard my knuckles go white as I fight to remain in control and to not make a noise. I bite my lip as Matt increases the pressure on my clit, pushing me closer to the edge.

He leans closer to me again and whispers in my ear, "How's this for something to think about?" he teases me.

"Mmhmm," I say, not trusting myself to formulate actual words.

He keeps working my clit, and I feel my climax rushing through me, spreading fire through my body. It's so hard to not react, to not scream out loud, move or even change my expression, but I manage it. As waves of pleasure rush through me, I sit still, my eyes fixed on a spot ahead of me.

I swallow hard as my climax slams through my body. My grip on the edge of the table becomes tighter. A rush of warmth leaves my pussy, soaking into my panties. I close my eyes for a moment and the restaurant is gone as fire explodes through my stomach. I force my eyes open again, not daring to forget my surroundings for even a second longer.

Matt pulls his fingers away as my orgasm starts to fade, leaving behind a tingly, sated feeling that leaves me breathless and feeling alive. I shake my head at Matt as he grins at me. "I can't believe you did that," I scold playfully.

"Really? Because I didn't hear you complaining."

I laugh, a soft laugh that comes out as more of a rush of air than an actual laugh. "Oh, I'm not complaining that you did it. I'm complaining that you stopped."

His eyes open wider for a moment and then he turns away from me. "Waiter? Can we get the bill please?" he shouts.

I smile to myself, covering my mouth with my hand to hide it. Matt isn't the only one who is full of surprises. Oh, no. Two can play that game.

The bill comes and Matt ignores my insistence on paying half of it. I know I've just told him I'm not exactly rolling in it, but I also told him I like to pay my own way. We're still talking about it as we head towards the door.

"I really don't expect you to pay for all of this," I say.

"I know," he replies. "But here's the thing. I have a plan."

I raise my eyebrow. "And what's that?"

"Well, I know now you have a thing about not relying on anyone else. So that means the next date is on you. Which means there has to be one." He grins.

I finally relax and smile up at him, feeling my cheeks flushing. He wants a second date.

Matt nods to the doormen as we leave the restaurant.

I start to head in the direction of the station but Matt catches my arm. "No train tonight."

Before I can ask why, a sleek yellow Porsche pulls to a stop by the curb. The valet from the restaurant gets out and holds the door open. Matt steps towards the car.

"This is yours?" I ask suspiciously.

"No." He laughs. "My brother's. He lent it to me when I told him I was trying to impress a girl." He holds the door open for me.

I smile at him as I get in. The seats in the car are low and I'm careful not to flash my panties as I slip into the seat. I watch Matt walk around the front of the car, admiring his ass in his jeans.

He thanks the valet and gets into the car.

"So..." I grin at him. "Your brother. Is he single?"

"Oh, you are so going to pay for that." Matt laughs as he pulls away from the curb. The engine is smooth and ultra quiet. "At least I can tell him the car worked. Even if not in the way I wanted it to."

He's heading in the direction of my dorm room, but I am definitely not ready for him to drop me off. I am tipsy and loving it, and I'm loving Matt's company. I quickly realize that I drank all of the wine but half a glass with dinner. "Oh, come on Matt. You had me the moment you touched me in the restaurant," I say, looking at him sideways. I run my tongue suggestively over my lips. "The car is a nice touch though. It means we have somewhere to elaborate on that."

Matt groans longingly and turns quickly, heading away from my dorm and I smile to myself. I don't know where we're heading and I don't much care. All I know is he's not taking me home yet.

Chapter Thirteen

MATT

*Y*et again, I've had to lie to Callie and I hate myself for it. We're having a fantastic night, made all the better by her not so subtle hint that she wants to end the night on a high note, and for me at least, it's marred by my lies.

But I can hardly tell her this car is mine. I can hardly tell her how I know the owner of The Herb Garden. I did tell her some truths though. I really do love good food, and I really did get that from my mom. That has to be more important, right? It's certainly more real. The rest is just material stuff, window dressing. I showed Callie a real part of who I am tonight. I hope it's enough.

I pull my car into a deserted parking lot beside a closed shopping center. I turn to Callie. I don't have time to speak before she's unclicked her seat belt and leaned across to fit her lips perfectly over mine.

I reach up and touch her face, running my fingers over her porcelain smooth skin. Callie runs her hand down my chest as she kisses me. She tastes of wine and chocolate, sweet like her. And I know nothing else matters but the way I feel about her in this moment. This is real. More real than anything I've ever felt in my whole life.

I run my hands over Callie's body and pull her closer to me. She breaks our kiss and I take the opportunity to remove my own seat belt. She isn't gone from me for long. She clambers across the central console and sits on my lap straddling me. Her lips are back on mine in seconds. I put my arms around her waist, pulling her against me. I slip my hands beneath her dress and run them up her back and down her sides. She slips her tongue into my mouth and pushes her hands into my hair, grinding her hips against my lap.

My cock is as hard as iron, ready for this. I know Callie can feel it against her pussy as she rocks back and forth on me. Each movement makes my cock throb and I know I can't wait much longer before I am inside of her.

I reach down and open my jeans, still kissing Callie as I go. I pull my fly open and lift my ass enough to push my jeans and boxers down.

"Fuck me Matt," Callie says against my lips in a breathless voice.

I push her panties to one side and push my cock inside of her warm, wet pussy. She forces herself down onto my lap, taking my length, impaling herself on my cock as I claim her pussy. I moan as I feel her tight sheath gripping me, pulling me inside of her, deeper and deeper.

She begins to move up and down, her hands pressed on my shoulders, her head thrown back. I match her thrusts, slamming into her, enjoying how fucking tight she is. She clenches her muscles, making her pussy even tighter and my breath catches in my throat.

I reach up and push the straps off her shoulders, exposing her pert breasts. Her nipples are hard, pointing at me. I knead her breasts and then I rub my thumbs over her hard nipples, watching them flatten and then spring back to erect. I squeeze them between my fingers, rolling them and tugging on them. Callie moans as I play with them, her breath becoming a fast pant as she moves on me. I can feel how slippery and wet she is and it's hard for me to hold myself back. I can feel my orgasm building and I know it won't be much longer before I explode.

I reach down and push my thumb between Callie's lips, finding her clit. I rub my thumb over it, feeling how swollen it is, how close she is to coming. I massage it roughly, hard and fast, pushing her over the edge. I feel her pussy clenching around my cock, pinning me in place for a moment. My own climax is almost upon me now, and with one final hard thrust, I come with Callie.

Her pussy is going wild, clenching and relaxing, clenching and relaxing, as I spurt into her, my cock twitching erratically as the heat of my coming slams through my body. I am being pressed back in the seat with the intensity of my climax and I can feel my face twisting as the pleasure floods me. I moan Callie's name as I spurt inside of her again, her clenching pussy milking me, pulling every last drop of cum from my cock.

My climax begins to fade as Callie calls out my name. I wrap my arms around her waist and hold her as her body stiffens and her pussy clenches once more. She collapses forwards as her orgasm fades, leaning against me, her head laid on my shoulder. I hold her tightly as we pant in unison, fighting to get our breaths back.

When we get ourselves under control, Callie lifts her head from my shoulder and smiles at me. She kisses me softly on the lips and then she moves back into her own seat.

I instantly miss her warming presence on my lap and I know I never want to let this girl go. Reluctantly, I lift my ass from the seat again to pull my boxers and jeans back into place. "So... you still want my brother's number?" I ask her as I fasten my jeans up.

"Nah. I'll pass." She grins at me. "The car is used goods now."

Chapter Fourteen

CALLIE

I smile to myself as I leave my dorm room to meet Matt. I texted him this morning to see if he was ready for date two. He was. I wouldn't tell him what I had planned. I told him it was a surprise. I'm a little nervous now if I'm honest. The date isn't exactly anything fancy and I hope he's not expecting too much.

I spent hours this morning wracking my brain trying to work out what the hell we should do. When it finally came to me, I got straight online to try and book something.

My plan is a visit to a local park, where we will have delicious chicken sandwiches and cold coke. And then I've booked us a cooking lesson. Matt made it clear to me how much he loves food and cooking, so I think we'll have a lot of fun. I hope I haven't read him all wrong and he hates the idea.

The park isn't far from my dorm room, a ten minute walk, but by the time I reach the park gates, I've talked myself in and out of the date idea so many times that my head is spinning. I don't even notice Matt coming towards me until he's right by my side.

He laughs when he sees my startled expression. "What? Did you expect me to stand you up?"

"No, but you might end up wishing you had."

"And why would you think that? Don't I strike you as the outdoors type?" Matt grins.

"Not exactly." I let out a small chuckle, relaxing a little as I lead the way into the park. "But it's not that. It's — well, what we're going to be doing isn't going to be anything fancy."

"You know, I'm starting to wish I'd had just taken you to McDonalds last night." Matt smiles.

"Me too," I admit.

"If it makes you feel any better, with my discount, the meal we had last night was about the same price as two Big Mac meals," he says.

It shouldn't matter, but his admission actually does make me feel better and I relax further. When Matt slips his fingers in between mine, I stop telling myself he's going to hate the date and decide instead to just enjoy his company. If all else fails, I can always take him back to my dorm room and have my wicked way with him.

I lead Matt past a small duck pond and along a winding path through the flower beds. We pass a playing field full of young boys playing soccer, families picnicking together and couples walking dogs. It's a beautiful spot, one I would normally consider a good place to sit and soak up the atmosphere and watch the world go by, but not today. Today, I want us to be somewhere a little more private. We keep walking until we come to a gated archway. I open the gate and we step through it into the vegetable garden. It's quiet here, like I knew it would be. It's where I come when I want to escape the noise of the city for a time, and I'm pleased it hasn't let me down now. Matt and I make our way through the vegetable plot until we reach the other side of it where a solitary picnic bench sits.

"Here we are," I say, gesturing to the bench.

I wish I had a picnic basket, but I don't. What sort of student does? Instead, I pull the Prosecco and the strawberries from the shopping bag I've been holding. I go and put the bag in the trash and come back to the table. I pull a corkscrew out of my purse and hand it to Matt who grins at me. He shakes his head and opens the Prosecco with a flourish without taking the corkscrew. Of course. What was I thinking? Obviously, I was more nervous than I thought when I collected the things I thought we would need.

I watch as a thin spool of what looks like steam comes from the bottle's neck. No foam spills out and I nod to Matt, impressed that he hasn't wasted any.

"This isn't my first rodeo Callie." He laughs when he sees my approving expression.

I soon spot the first problem. Apparently, this is my first rodeo. Or at least it would seem that way as I bounce from issue to issue.

"I didn't think to bring any glasses," I say.

Matt shrugs and takes a swig from the bottle. He smiles and offers it to me. I laugh and take a sip. The bubbles tickle my mouth and throat and the warming effect as I swallow, calms me. Matt doesn't seem to be judging me for my total lack of bottle opening knowledge and the lack of glassware isn't bothering him, so why should I let it bother me? It's actually kind of romantic in a way to share the bottle this way, my lips on the spot his occupied seconds before mine. We sit eating the strawberries, chatting about nothing in particular.

"You know Callie, you didn't have to worry about this," Matt says. "It's perfect."

"This is just the warm up," I tell him.

He raises an eyebrow then winks suggestively, looking around him in an exaggerated manner. "Really? We're going to do it in the shed?" He raises his eyebrows up and down.

I laugh. "Get your mind out of the gutter. I mean I have something else planned."

"Do tell," he says.

I pause. I wanted to keep it as a surprise, but I'm afraid if I give it too much build up, it won't come even close to living up to the unintentional hype I'll be creating. "I've booked us a cooking lesson. At the community center down the road."

Matt grins and squeezes my knee beneath the table. "You know me so well," he purrs.

I bite my tongue so I don't blurt out what I'm thinking and ruin the mood. I don't know him at all. Well, nothing except this one thing. Maybe though, when he sees me making an effort to plan things I know he'll enjoy, he'll open up and tell me more. "What can I say? It's a skill." I smile. "It's called listening."

Matt laughs and bites into another strawberry. What I wouldn't give to be that strawberry right now. But we can't do anything here. No matter how much I want to. This part of the park is quiet, but it's still a public place. And despite Matt's joke, there's no way in hell I'm doing anything in a dusty, cobwebby shed.

We're well over half way down the bottle of Prosecco and the strawberries are gone, when out of nowhere, the heavens open and cold, fat drops of rain begin to land on us. I jump up, a squeal escaping me.

Matt laughs at my reaction, but he gets to his feet too. "Maybe it's time to start making our way to somewhere a bit drier." he laughs.

The rain is pouring down. I'm already soaked to my skin. I can feel my hair plastering itself to my head, but I can't help but laugh. Matt isn't faring any better than me. His t-shirt is sticking to his body, showing me his clearly defined abs and pecs. His hair is flattened by the rain, inviting me to run my hands through it and muss it up. Ok, so he's fairing slightly better than me then.

He gathers up the trash and takes it to the trash, and then he comes back and grabs my hand. We walk quickly towards the exit of the park, laughing and passing the bottle back and forth until it's empty and we deposit it in the next trash we come to.

"I bet teenagers get the blame for that one." Matt grins.

I nod in agreement. I feel like a teenager again when I'm with Matt, so maybe they won't be entirely wrong. The rain pours down heavier and we begin to run. I hold my hand uselessly over my head. I don't know why. It's far too late to attempt to keep my hair dry. We jog through the park, watching as the families from the field frantically pack up as small children laugh and dance in the rain, ignoring their parent's calling them to come on.

We run from the park, dash across the road and we finally reach the community center and burst through the doors, both of us laughing as we enter.

The room is silent as we enter and suddenly, I feel all eyes on us. I stop laughing abruptly, feeling my face turning red. The room is filled with parents and their children and they're all staring at us. "I'm sorry," I manage to say. "Can you point us in the direction of the cooking lesson please?"

A stern looking woman steps forward.

"This is the cooking lesson. How old is your child?"

"Child?" I ask.

"Well yes. It's a parent and child cooking class."

I just shake my head as I am seized by laughter again. "I think — I think I booked the wrong class," I manage to stutter out and look over at Matt who is laughing beside me and he just shrugs and shakes his head in an, *I'm as lost as you are* gesture.

I can't stay here any longer, under the angry glares of parents and the curious stares of their children. I am very much aware of the bedraggled look of myself and the wine fumes emanating from us. Not a great look around children.

I stutter out another apology to the woman and lead Matt back out into the street. At least, the rain is easing off a little now. It's too late for my hair or makeup, but it's nice to not have to jog anymore.

"Well that was interesting," Matt comments.

"I can't believe I booked a parent and child cooking class!" I laugh.

"It sure puts a new slant on the idea of you calling me *Daddy*," Matt grins.

I elbow him playfully in the ribs. "Eww," I say, wrinkling my nose.

"Hey, I'm not the one booking parent and child classes and calling it a date," he reminds me.

I groan. "This has been an utter disaster hasn't it?" I say. "The rain, the fucked up booking."

"It's a story to tell our kids one day. I'll use it as an example to show them that this is why we don't let Mommy make the plans."

His tone is light and teasing, but I can't help but focus on him talking about our future. Our kids. "You want kids?" I ask, trying to keep my voice even.

"Sure. Don't you?" he asks.

"Well yeah I guess. One day."

"I'm sorry," Matt says. "I've come on way too strong haven't I? I was just kidding Callie. It's not like I was planning on proposing to you tomorrow or anything."

I feel a tingling in my stomach at the thought of it. It's ridiculous. Of course, he isn't going to propose and even if he did, it's not like I would say yes. We barely know each other. But still, it was nice to hear him planning our future together. I smile at him, not wanting it to be awkward between us, and not wanting him to think for a second he's scared me off. "I was just thinking that if you tell our kids about this date, I swear I'll string you up," I say with a laugh.

"And what are you going to use to bribe me into staying silent?" he asks.

I happen to glance up as we walk and I spot the movie theatre and an idea comes into my head. Maybe we can still turn this date around. "Popcorn," I blurt out, pulling him to a stop and nodding towards the theatre.

"Works for me," he says.

We step into the theatre and I excuse myself to go to the bathroom to try to make myself look vaguely human again. I quickly pull a comb through my hair and squeeze the excess water from it. My makeup is beyond repair, so rather than trying to reapply it, I just wipe away the black mascara streaks that sit beneath my eyes. It's not great; certainly not a look I would choose for a date. But it'll have to do.

I go back to the lobby to find Matt looking at the listings.

If he notices I look a complete mess, he's enough of a gentleman to not point it out to me. "If we want to go in now, we have two choices," he says, pointing to the board.

I take a look. A romantic comedy that I don't think Matt will much enjoy and I know I won't. The other option looks good though. It's a scary movie about a haunted house. "How about that one?" I say, pointing to the scary movie.

"Are you just saying that because you think I'll hate the other one?" Matt questions.

"Honestly Matt, I'm saying it because I think I'll hate the other one," I declare.

"You have no idea how relieved that makes me." He smiles and sets off towards the ticket counter.

I run a couple of steps to get in front of him. "My turn, remember."

"You bought the Prosecco," he points out.

"Yup. And now I'm buying the movie tickets."

He looks like he's about to argue.

I raise my eyebrow at him.

He closes his mouth and makes a motion like he's drawing a zipper over his lips.

"That's better." I buy two tickets to the movie, a large popcorn and a coke to share. We time it perfectly, stepping into the theatre as the trailers end and the movie begins. We take our seats.

We nibble on popcorn as we watch the movie. Although we can't really chat here, it's nice to feel Matt's arm against mine, his leg against mine. I consider exaggerating my fear at the jumpy parts of the movie so that he'll hold me, but I decide I don't want him to think I'm a total wimp. I find myself becoming engrossed in the movie, although I still notice every time Matt's fingers brush mine as we reach for the popcorn. When the movie ends, I turn to Matt. "Pretty good wasn't it?"

"Good enough that I didn't want to disturb you and do this..." He kisses me.

His lips are buttery and sweet and my stomach flutters as his tongue pokes into my mouth. My body responds to his touch, and I feel myself shifting closer to him, my pussy getting wet as we kiss. I pull away, I have to before I can let myself go any further. I sit for a moment, content looking into Matt's eyes. "How on earth do you have this effect on me?" I whisper. I've never been with anyone who has me on the edge of losing control with just a kiss, or a whispered word. Even a look.

"It's my natural charm." He smirks.

I laugh and swat at him.

He ducks, laughing. "Seriously Callie, I don't know. But I do know you have the same effect on me. I can't even look at you without wanting to take you home and pleasure you all night long."

My pussy clenches at his words and I moan low in my throat. I want nothing more than that myself. "Don't... I have work soon."

"Skip it." Matt grins. "Call in sick."

"I... I can't do that. I'm sorry. I have this rule, where I don't date co-workers. Clearly I've broken it, but I can't let what we have affect work. I just can't."

He kisses the tip of my nose. "I get it. The restaurant is lucky to have you. And so am I."

Chapter Fifteen

CALLIE

*I*t's been almost two weeks since Matt and I went on our disastrous date which actually turned out pretty well, all things considered. We've spent a lot of time together since that day, and while we haven't actually come out and said it, we're pretty much a couple. When we're not at work, we go out together, or Matt comes and hangs out in my dorm room. We watch scary movies, old cheesy slasher ones, and laugh at the terrible effects and the over the top acting.

Everyone at the restaurant has worked out that we're together, although when I'm asked about it, I neither confirm nor deny it. I don't let Matt distract me at work, as hard as it is to focus on anything but him, but the chemistry between us is so obvious, anyone would know there was something between us. Sasha is constantly quizzing me for details, and the others are always making jokes about us. Even Marco seems to have noticed something is there between Matt and me. I was most worried about Marco finding out. I thought he would make my life at work even more of a living hell if he knew I was dating Matt, but instead, he's backed off me a lot. He's not nice to me; that would be too much to ask, but he keeps his distance and that's more than enough for me. I guess he still remembers the last time Matt nearly punched him and he knows better than to bring that on himself again.

I am barely through the door for my shift tonight when James beckons me over. "Marco wants to see you in his office."

"Okay," I say as my heart sinks. What fresh hell is this? There's bound to be some sort of customer complaint, whether real or imagined. Something minor that Marco will make a huge big deal out of. I head for his office, steeling myself for what's coming. I might as well get it over with now instead of spending the first half of my shift with it hanging over my head until he realizes I'm here.

I head down the hallway and tap on his office door.

"Come in," he shouts.

I open the door and poke my head around it. "James said you wanted to see me."

He nods and gestures for me to come in.

I enter and move towards Marco's desk, purposely keeping the door ajar. As I move towards the desk, my eyes are automatically drawn to his couch. I bite the inside of my lip to stop myself from smiling. I don't know what's coming, but I do know that if Marco gets the impression I'm happy about something, he'll do his best to ruin it. He can't ruin this. He can't take away from what happened on that couch. But I really can't be bothered with his attitude, so I hide my joy. I take a seat opposite him, being careful to pull my skirt right down and keep my knees pressed shut as I do.

"How do you think your performance has been recently Callie?" Marco asks me.

It's a loaded question and I consider my options. I think my performance has been just fine, but if I say that, Marco will accuse me of being arrogant and find faults with my performance just to try and upset me. If I say anything even remotely negative about my performance, he'll pounce on it, happy to agree with me. I have a feeling this is about Matt. Marco has obviously grown bored of keeping his distance and he's ready to accuse me of being distracted at work because of what's happening between Matt and me. It's not true, but that won't stop Marco from using it against me.

I decide to be honest. If I'm going to be berated, I'm going to fight my corner, and I can't do that if I tell Marco I don't think my performance has been good. "Good," I say. "I think I have a good rapport with the customers and I think we're a good team that are usually on top of service."

Marco nods slowly. He puts his hands together on his desk. He smiles at me; a smile I can't read.

"I'm inclined to agree with you Callie. Which is why I'm promoting you. You will be a shift supervisor, which means that you'll be the head waitress on your shifts and it will be up to you to ensure service runs well. Of course, it means extra money too – an extra 3.50 per hour."

Admittedly, I don't like the way Marco tells me this is happening instead of offering me the chance to accept or refuse the promotion, but honestly, I don't care. It's just semantics. I am taken aback by the news, but I try my best not to show it.

Marco smiles again, a more normal smile this time. "You don't look very happy about it," he says.

"Oh no, I am... I just wasn't expecting it is all. Thank you."

He nods to me. "The promotion and raise are effective immediately. Don't let me down Callie," he says, signalling that our conversation is over by turning to his computer and beginning to type.

"I won't." I stand up to leave. I turn back when I reach his office door. "Thanks again."

He doesn't even look up from the screen.

I wonder momentarily why he's given me the promotion. I mean I'm far from his favorite waitress and it's not like I've been here the longest amount of time. I tell myself to stop berating myself and to stop being negative. I'm good at my job. I'm organized, and when it matters, people listen to me. Obviously, Marco is better at his job than I gave him credit for, and he's put his own prejudices aside to make a fair decision about the promotion.

As I reach the restaurant floor, Matt appears while going in the opposite direction.

"Ice run?" I ask, unable to keep the smile from my face.

"Potatoes." He grins back. "What are you so happy about?"

I look around quickly to make sure no one is watching us and then I step back into the corridor out of sight, pulling Matt with me. "I've just been promoted to shift supervisor." I can't keep the excitement out of my voice.

"That's great news Callie." Matt grins.

"You don't seem too surprised." I say with a frown.

"I'm only surprised it's taken this long. You deserve this Callie. You're a credit to this place."

I beam at him.

He quickly leans in and brushes his lips across mine. "After work, we're celebrating."

"Doing what?" I ask.

"Leave that to me." He gives me a wink.

I hurry onto the restaurant floor, wondering what Matt is going to do. Maybe I'll finally get an invite to his place. We spend all of our time out and about or in my dorm room, and never once have I been to Matt's place. As much as I want to relax and give myself to Matt completely, I still hold myself back from him a little bit. I still feel like he's hiding something from me, and his reluctance to take me to his place only confirms it for me.

My shift flies by, and before I know it, as usual, Matt and I are left to lock up.

"So where are we going?" I ask as we leave the restaurant.

"You'll see." He leads me along the street.

I follow willingly. I expect us to go to the diner we went to on our first night together, but Matt passes it without a glance, leading me to a hotel a couple of doors down.

"Are we having drinks in here?" I ask as Matt gestures for me to step inside.

"Better than that," he says close to my ear. "We're having a room here."

My stomach flutters with butterflies as we make our way across the lobby. I know what's coming next. I know how we'll celebrate and I am more than ready for it. I hang back, watching Matt from a distance as he checks us in. I wonder again, why he didn't just take me to his place.

I know it was only a few weeks ago he was talking about our kids, but I can't help but think he's not really serious about us. That would explain why he never takes me home with him. Why he never reveals more than a snippet here and there of himself to me. Because he doesn't want to get invested in something that's just casual.

I'm still trying to work out if I'm okay with that or not when Matt comes over to me, waving a card key in front of my face. I smile up at him and the look on his face, the look that says he's hungry for me. I don't know if I'm okay with a casual relationship going forward. I'll have to think about it. But I'm as sure as hell okay with it tonight.

We head for the elevator. Matt presses the call button. As we wait for it to arrive, I can feel my clit throbbing, my imagination running wild about what we will get up to in our room.

The elevator pings, bringing me back to reality. Matt and I step inside of it. I am kind of disappointed when another couple joins us in the elevator. It would have been nice to have started what I know is coming, but I can wait another few minutes. I'll have to.

We leave the elevator when the doors pings open again on the fourth floor.

Matt grins at me.

It's a grin that sends fire through my body and makes my pussy wet as we practically run down the corridor to our room.

Matt runs the card through the slot. It seems to take forever for the light to turn green, but eventually, it does. Matt pushes the door open and holds it wide so I can step inside the room ahead of him.

The room looks nice, all white with purple curtains and a purple runner across the bed. That's all I get a chance to really take in before I hear the door slam shut behind Matt. I turn and fall into his arms.

Our lips meet in a fiery kiss that has me gasping for breath. Our hands are all over each other as we fumble with each other's buttons. By the time we reach the bed, I'm naked from the waist up and Matt is wearing only his boxer shorts. I take a moment to study him, to take in his washboard stomach. I feel a rush of desire at the sight of him.

He goes to push me backwards onto the bed and I dart out of his reach. He frowns at me as I grin and fall to my knees before him. He gasps in a breath as I pull his boxer shorts down to his ankles. He kicks them away as I take in the glorious sight of his hard cock. I reach out and run my fingernails over his inner thighs. He gasps again and I lean forward. I grasp his cock by the base and pull it towards me, flicking my tongue over the tip, enjoying the salty taste.

I purse my lips, taking the very tip of him into my mouth and licking over him like a lollipop. He moans low in his throat. The noise is so full of lust that I feel a rush of wetness coming from my pussy.

I open my lips and suck Matt's cock into my mouth, relishing the taste of it, the feel of it against my tongue. I begin to move my lips up and down the length, my head bobbing up and down as my tongue glides along it. I reach around Matt and grip his ass cheeks, pulling him closer to me, taking his cock deeper into my mouth.

I feel like I am about to gag, but I take a steadying breath through my nose and the feeling passes. I love having him in my mouth, filling me up. I suck him hard, making him gasp once more, and then I plunge my head down, taking all of him into the back of my throat. I come back up a little and move one hand off his ass, gripping his cock. I move my fist up and down in time with my mouth, flicking my tongue across his sensitive tip again.

I know he's getting close to orgasming. I can feel his cock throbbing in my grip. I release his cock, standing up, needing to feel him inside of me before he comes. I look him in the eye and run my tongue over my lips, savouring the taste of him. His eyes are glassy with lust and when he pushes me towards the bed again, this time, I don't try to stop him.

I land on my back, my legs hanging over the edge of the bed. Matt takes hold of me by my knees and flips me onto my front. I take my weight on my feet and hands, bending over the bed, knowing he is getting one hell of a view of my dripping wet pussy.

Matt wastes no time. I can feel the tip of his cock moving through my slit, and then he slams into me, stretching me open, claiming my pussy, and making me gasp in a tortured breath. He pulls almost all of the way out of me and then he slams into me again. I brace myself on the palms of my hands, pushing back against him, wanting to feel all of him inside of me.

He moves slower now, long, smooth strokes that make me moan in delight as his cock rubs over my g-spot. His hand moves across my body, reaching around to the front of me and finding my clit. He massages it in time with his thrusts, slow and steady, driving me wild and making me want more.

"Oh my God, Matt," I moan.

I need him to bring me over the edge, to release the climax that is moving to the surface of me. I feel like I am swimming through warm, thick syrup and I need him to throw me a lifeline, to pull me through the tranquil waves and into the choppy water my climax will bring.

He ups his pace, moving his fingers faster and harder across my clit. It's as though he's read my mind. My breath catches in my throat as my orgasm explodes through my whole body, making me cry out. He continues to play with my clit as I move through the heady orgasm, and I can feel another orgasm building inside of me even before the first one has fully come out.

I am slammed headlong into the most intense pleasure I have ever felt in my life. My whole body feels my climax. My pussy goes wild, clenching and relaxing and my clit throbs so fast it's almost a vibration. My stomach turns wildly, and my heart hammers in my chest so hard I'm almost afraid it is trying to break loose. My skin tingles, a light tickling sensation that seems to be on the inside of my skin rather than the outside. The sensation makes my nerves fire up and send pulses of pleasure down my veins and along through my bones.

My eyes close, red flashes of light exploding like fireworks on the insides of my eyelids. My ears ring, a not unpleasant sound as the blood pumps through my body with an undulating whooshing sound.

I can't breathe, can't move, as every muscle in my body contracts tightly and goes rigid. My back arches almost painfully, the tendons in my neck straining as another wave of pleasure slams through me, leaving my mouth hanging open in a silent O of ecstasy.

Still Matt slams into me, bringing more fire with every stroke of his cock. My eyes roll back in their sockets, and for a second, there's only darkness, and I'm floating in a void of nothingness, just a giant nerve ending built solely to feel the overwhelming pleasure.

I can finally breath again and I suck in a huge breathe that burns my dry throat and aches my lungs. I gasp and pant as Matt continues to thrust into me. I feel my knees buckle, and Matt's fingers leave my clit, catching me. He holds my hips, keeping my legs upright, pulling me back onto his cock over and over again, slamming against my cervix and pushing me to open further for him.

My elbows give up and I fall, landing face down on the bed. The silken feeling of the duvet cover against my cheek does nothing to soothe the raging hormones that flood me.

Finally, I feel Matt tense up, his cock twitching inside of me.

"You are mine Callie," he says, and then he comes, a hot spurt of liquid filling my pussy. He moans my name as his cock twitches again, and then he pulls out of me and lowers me onto the bed.

I manage to roll onto my side as he flops onto the bed beside me. We lay facing each other, looking into each other's eyes as we pant for breath.

"Holy shit," I manage when I feel like I can trust my voice again. "That was fucking awesome."

"That was just a warm up Callie." Matt winks.

I don't think I can take anymore, but my pussy disagrees. I feel the tingling starting up again, the rush of warm liquid, and I know Matt is right. We're just getting started. He shuffles closer to me, and our lips meet once more. Instantly, I feel my pussy responding, flooding me with a wash of wetness. My clit throbs almost painfully and my pussy aches, the tender flesh battered by Matt's incessant thrusts, but I don't care about that. I just want to feel Matt inside of me again.

I hook my leg over his hips and push him onto his back, straddling him. I lean forward, kissing him softly then holding my lips just out of his reach. He reaches up and takes hold of my shoulders, pulling my face back down to his. I move slightly from side to side, letting my hard nipples graze over Matt's chest. He moans as I move my hips, running my slit over his hardening cock. I can feel it growing harder as I continue to move.

I break our kiss and scoot backwards, placing my ass on Matt's thighs. I take his cock in one fist and begin to work him, moving my hand up and down him, slowly at first. He props himself up on his elbows and holds my gaze while I work him.

Seeing his lust filled eyes spurs me on and I begin to move faster.

Matt's mouth drops open and he moans again. He puts his head back, his fists bunching in the sheet beneath him. "Fuck Callie," he moans, a low growl filled with need that makes my pussy ache for him.

I scoot forwards again and keeping a grip on the base of his cock, I rub it through my lips. I gasp as it presses against my clit, sending an electric shock through my sensitive skin there. I move him back towards my pussy and lift my hips. I line him up and come down onto his cock, impaling myself with his length, stretching myself open wide to accommodate him.

I take him all the way in and then I begin to move up and down on him, slowly at first, long slow movements that pull him all of the way inside of me and then almost all of the way back out. His cock brushes over my g-spot with each stroke, pushing me closer to the edge.

I begin to speed up. Matt's eyes go to my breasts as I bounce up and down on top of him. He watches them eagerly and I reach up and fondle my nipples, bringing them to points. Matt moans again and I smile to myself. I run my tongue over my lips and then I bring two fingers to my mouth. I run my tongue over them, getting them nice and wet and then I press them between my other lips, massaging my clit with them.

I move on Matt's cock and play with my clit, throwing my head back and enjoying the sensations I am creating in my body. My orgasm creeps up slowly and then it slams through me, tightening my pussy and making me whimper with its intensity. I grit my teeth as my whole body is consumed by tingling ecstasy. My skin, my veins, every part of me comes alive, sending me into a climax that makes me scream out Matt's name.

As my orgasm fades, I pull my fingers away from myself. I lean forward slightly, pushing them into Matt's mouth. He sucks on my fingers, licking them clean and I up my pace again, short, fast strokes that make Matt grip the sheet again.

I know he's close now, I can feel his cock twitching inside of me, and I squeeze my pussy, holding his cock tightly in my grip. He shouts my name as he comes hard, his face twisted with pleasure as his warm cum fills me. I clench my pussy again, and I am rewarded with another moan, another spurt.

He reaches up for me and I collapse into his arms, panting for breath. He kisses my forehead as I lay beside him with my head on his chest. I run my nails slowly up and down his abs, relishing the rock hard feeling of them.

I never want this moment to end. I can feel my eyes starting to close as I lay still, listening to Matt's rhythmic breathing. I relax and let sleep take me.

I wake up to Matt's gentle kiss. It takes me a moment to work out where the hell I am, but it soon comes flooding back to me. We're in a hotel room. And we had the most mind blowing marathon of sex of my life before I passed out, exhausted from my orgasms. Matt made me come and come and come, and it looks like we're heading for round two. No complaints here.

I reach up and push my hands into Matt's hair as he kisses me.

He pulls back and smiles down at me. "We should go."

"Go? What time is it?" I ask.

"Almost seven. Do you have class today?"

"What day is it?" I ask, still a little confused.

"Friday." Matt smiles.

"Shit," I say, sitting up. "Yeah. I have a class in a couple of hours." I get up off the bed, as much as I want to stay there with Matt. I begin to collect up my clothes and put them on.

Matt makes no effort to move.

"Are you enjoying the show?" I ask with a grin.

"Oh yeah," Matt grins back at me. "But I have to say, I think I'd enjoy it more if those clothes were coming off instead of going on."

"We'll have to see what we can do about that after work tonight." I grin.

"Deal." Matt nods.

He finally moves only when I'm fully dressed again.

It's my turn to watch the show, and a fine show it is.

All too soon though, Matt is fully clothed. "Come on, I'll call a cab and drop you off."

I nod and he makes the call. We head downstairs and Matt checks us out and we go to wait on the curb for the Uber.

"So I was thinking maybe tonight we could spend the night at your place," I say.

"We'll see," he says, not looking at me.

I was right. He isn't as into me as I am him, and he wants this to be a casual thing. I'm really not sure I can do that. I'm kind of an all or nothing sort of a girl. But can I walk away from sex like that? "Why have I never been to your place? Do you have your ex-wife's body under the patio or something?" I ask, keeping my tone light.

"Yeah that's exactly it. What gave it away?" Matt jokes.

I laugh, but I feel like crying and I realize I'm not ready to let this go. "Seriously, why do we never go to your place Matt? Is it because you want to keep me at arm's length? Am I just a booty call to you?"

"Are you fucking kidding me Callie? You think that's all you are to me?"

"I don't know," I say, looking down at the ground, suddenly too embarrassed to meet his eye.

Matt reaches out and gently touches my chin, pushing my head up until I have no choice but to look at him. "You are mine Callie. I meant that. I really do care for you. Just about my place... it's complicated."

I can see the genuine look in his eye as he says he cares for me. I really want to believe this is real. I really think it is real. But I know he's still hiding something from me. I open my mouth to demand he tell me what it is once and for all, but before I can find the words, our Uber pulls up.

We get in and sit at opposite ends of the seat, both of us looking out of the window. I can't have this conversation with him in the back of an Uber, but I don't know what else to say to him. What else matters?

I feel warmth on my hand and I glance down to see Matt has wrapped my fingers in his. I glance at his face and he smiles sadly at me. The hurt on his face tells me that his feelings are real. And the rest?

Well, we can deal with that later.

I shuffle closer to him and he looks relieved as he gently lets go of my hand and wraps his arm around my shoulders. I rest my head on his shoulder, my hand on his knee. We ride the rest of the way to my dorm that way.

"See you tonight," I say as I get out of the Uber. "Thanks for the ride."

He grabs my hand through the window and pulls me towards him.

Laughing, I bend down and kiss him.

"See you tonight," he agrees. "I'll be counting down the minutes."

The Uber pulls away, leaving me with more questions than answers and a whole fucking host of feelings that I fear will lead to me getting very hurt. *How the hell did I get myself into this mess?*

Chapter Seventeen

CALLIE

riday's at school normally fly by. They're busy days with back to back lectures and the promise of the weekend looming closer helps to pass the day as well. But today has dragged by. I feel like I've lived a week for every hour that's passed. Even the interesting lectures felt like a drag. And it's all Matt's fault, because I just can't get him out of my head.

It doesn't help that every time I forget myself and move too quickly, I feel a throb through my tender clit. My pussy feels bruised, battered in the nicest possible way and the feeling keeps Matt very much in the forefront of my mind. For the first time ever, I find myself looking forward to going to work, so I can see him again.

Finally, the time comes for me to hop on my train and go to work. I know Matt won't be on the train because he starts earlier than me today, but I've waited all damn day to see him – the half hour train ride isn't going to kill me.

The train ride and the walk from the station to the restaurant pass by pretty uneventfully, my head filled with thoughts of Matt. I keep hearing him telling me I am his. I should probably be offended – I'm no one's property – but I'm not. I like the way it sounds. I like the way it made me feel warm inside. And yeah, I like the idea of being his. So sue me.

It raises a major question though. If Matt isn't keeping me at arm's length because he doesn't want this thing between us to become too serious, then what the hell is he hiding from me? I've been through every possibility I can think of, and none of them make any sense. I know I'm going to have to confront him again, but I don't want us to end up arguing. I don't want to lose him.

Why can't he just be honest with me dammit? Surely, that's not too much to ask. It's kind of the most basic requirement in a relationship that's going anywhere.

I push away the questions and the doubts as I walk across the parking lot to the staff entrance. I check my watch. I'm fifteen minutes early and even Marco can't moan about that. The instant I step inside, I hear shouting. I frown and pause, listening. It's coming from down the corridor, and it sounds like Marco and Matt are arguing.

I take my jacket off and hang it over one of the chairs in the breakroom. I sling my handbag over the same chair and move down the corridor. I know I shouldn't eavesdrop, but I can't help myself. And it's not like they're exactly being subtle, so they can't be too worried about the idea of someone overhearing them. As I move out of the break room, I realize just how loud they're shouting, and I think it's likely they can be heard on the restaurant floor. *Fantastic.*

I up my pace, ready to go in and tell them to keep it down a bit. I pause outside of the office door.

"What the fuck are you playing at Marco? You had no fucking right to do that," Matt shouts.

"Excuse me?" Marco yells back. "I think you'll find I'm the manager here and I have every right to do it. It's none of your business, and it would pay you to show me a bit of respect and stop swearing at me."

"Respect? Why would I respect you after the stunt you've pulled? Don't think I don't know the full fucking story Marco," Matt fires back.

I miss Marco's response as Sasha and two other waitresses appear from the restaurant floor.

"What's going on Callie? We can hear them out in the restaurant. The diners are starting to notice," Sasha says.

I shake my head, shrugging my shoulders. I have no idea what's going on, but I've heard enough. I knock on the office door, not expecting to receive an answer. I push the door open and go in. "Guys, can you keep it down a bit or take it outside? The diners can hear you."

"Stay the fuck out of this Callie!" Marco snaps.

"Don't you dare talk to her like that," Matt shouts. "You know what? Pack your shit up. You're fired."

My jaw drops. Matt has gone way too far this time.

"I'm fired? That's funny. I think you'll find you're the one who is fired. I don't know who the fuck sent you here or why, and I don't care. You're done here Matt. Get the fuck out of here right now."

Matt is suddenly the picture of quiet fury. He reaches into his pocket and shows Marco something about the size of a business card.

Marco's whole demeanor changes. The anger goes out of him and he sits down heavily in his chair. "I..."

"I don't want to hear it," Matt interrupts. "Like I said before, don't think I don't know the full story. You have two choices Marco. You can resign right now and leave quietly. Or..."

"Ok, I'll leave," Marco interrupts him. "I'm so sorry. I just —"

"I said I don't want to hear it," Matt says again. "Get out. Your belongings will be forwarded on to you and I will expect your resignation letter to reach head office within the next hour."

Marco stands up quickly, nodding. His face is still pale, and he looks like he's defeated.

I can't for the life of me work out what's going on. What does Matt know that has scared Marco so badly? And how does Matt have the authority to fire Marco?

Marco starts to walk towards his office door.

Matt turns and seems to realize he has an audience for the first time.

I try to catch his eye but he won't even look at me.

"Sasha. Harriet. Would you ladies be so kind as to see that Marco leaves the premises please? If he gives you any trouble, come and find me," Matt says.

Sasha and Harriet both nod mechanically, looking as shocked as I am by the scene we've just witnessed.

"I won't be any trouble," Marco says. "I really am sorry about this. About everything."

No one responds to him. He heads towards the staff entrance, Harriet and Sasha following him. I know Sasha will quiz him once they're out of ear shot, so maybe we'll get some answers as to what's going on. For now though, I'm going to try and get some answers out of Matt.

"The rest of you go back to work. And please apologize to the diners for the interruption," Matt says.

I realize a couple of the other wait staff are hanging around in the hallway behind me, but they quickly scurry back to the diners, leaving Matt and I alone.

"What happened?" I ask.

"Marco fired James. He shouldn't have done that." His voice is low, full of anger.

I feel a flash of fear go through me. He made it sound like a threat, like Marco is going to come to some sort of harm. "Why —"

Matt walks towards the office door. "I'm sorry Callie, I have to make a phone call." He storms out through the dining area of the restaurant.

Leaving me standing open mouthed watching his back as he strides quickly away. I can see the tension in his shoulders, and I wonder again what the fuck just happened.

Why does Matt care this much if James was fired? And what does he have over Marco that made him so compliant? It must have been something to do with that card Matt showed Marco. He must have something on him, and he's black-mailing him.

I know I should be glad Marco is gone from the restaurant, gone from my life. And I am. But I can't just let it go at that. I have to know what exactly I am getting into with Matt.

*a*s I storm out of the restaurant, I can feel eyes on me. Callie's eyes, the eyes of all of the staff, and most likely the eyes of a fair few of the diners as well. I know once I leave, the silence will end and everyone will have an opinion on what just happened. The only opinion I care about is Callie's. I really do owe her an explanation, but first, I have to try and fix this mess. I just hope she's still open to hearing what I have to say after that.

I can't believe I let myself lose control that way, but Marco went too fucking far, especially when he swore at Callie and I just saw red. Who the fuck does he think he is? Some glorified little shit who thinks he's more clever than everyone around him and has a right to just betray people and do whatever the fuck he likes. Well, at least that's over. He has found out the hard way that isn't the case.

I lean back against the wall around the side of the restaurant. I close my eyes for a moment, trying to calm down and come up with some sort of a plan. It doesn't matter how I spin this in my head. The first step I have to take is obvious. I really do need to make a phone call. A phone call I'm absolutely dreading having to make.

With a loud sigh, I pull my phone out and scroll through my contacts. I hesitate for a moment before hitting call. I've really fucked this up and this call is going to make me feel like absolute shit. I have let my emotions affect me, something I swore to myself I wouldn't do, and explaining that is going to be a low moment for me. I was trusted to do a job here, and I've fucked it up. Just like he was worried I would. I insisted I could do it, and eventually he put his trust in me. And look where that's gotten us.

I can't put the call off forever though, and already the gossip mill will be turning. The only thing worse than making this call will be someone else beating me to it. At least if he hears it from me, I can tell him how I plan to fix it. The problem is, I have no idea how to fix it. I guess I'll just have to wing it.

I hit call, my stomach rolling as I wait for the call to be answered.

"Matt? What's up? There's an issue I'm dealing with here that requires my full attention. Can this wait?"

"Not really," I say.

"Then spit it out. But for the love of God, don't tell me you've messed this up."

Oh fuck. This is going to be even worse than I thought.

*A*s I make my way onto the restaurant floor after Matt storms away, two things hit me. Firstly, with Marco gone, and me as the shift supervisor, that means I'm in charge, at least for the minute, and I have to be the one to pull this all back together and get everyone working properly again, instead of standing around gossiping. Secondly, I cross my fingers that Marco moved quickly on informing HR about my promotion, otherwise, that's gone along with him and I'm back to just being a waitress again, after less than twenty-four hours in my new job.

"Ok guys, show's over," I say. "Let's try and turn this shift around and have a great service."

The wait staff grumble but they move off and at least make it look like they're busy. The order for one of my tables is up, so I go to collect the meals and deliver them. I'm glad for the moment of activity. It means I can't get pulled into the gossip, even though I'm dying to know if anyone knows what's going on.

I move through the dining room, taking a few more orders out to hungry diners, taking a bill to one of my tables and cleaning down some empty tables in my section. Sasha beckons me over as I make my way back to her.

She's standing polishing the silverware, a sure fire sign she wants to gossip because the silverware is always polished before it even gets put out into the dining room. The staff use it as an excuse to stand and chat while still looking busy to any casual observers.

"What's up?" I ask as I reach her.

"What's up? Are you on another planet Callie? I mean what could I possibly want to talk about right now?" Sasha says.

I roll my eyes. "I have no idea what's going on," I tell her.

"Yeah right," Sasha says. "So your boyfriend didn't tell you in advance this was going to happen? Who is he really Callie? How did he manage to get Marco to just leave?"

"I honestly have no idea," I say.

She must see the genuine confusion on my face. She frowns. "Don't you kind of think you should know? I mean you're dating the guy. I don't know who he really is or why he's really here, but he's clearly not just another waiter."

Her words confirm everything I've been thinking myself. I'm not paranoid. This is weird. I deflect her question by asking one of my own, "You left with Marco. What did he say was happening?"

"Nothing," she replies. "Harriet and I tried to get it out of him, but he just point blank refused to tell us anything. He didn't even try to make something up, he just remained completely silent, looking through us like we weren't even there."

"Nice to know whatever happened seemed to make him see the error of treating people like crap then." I grin.

Sasha laughs. "Marco will always be that asshole. It's just the way he is. But Matt seems different, so I'm willing to bet there's a good reason for what he did. Look it's quietening down. I'll watch your section. Go and find out what's going on," she urges me.

"How? I don't even know where Matt is," I point out.

It's Sasha's turn to roll her eyes. "God Callie, I hope you never decide to become any kind of investigator. He's around the side of the building. Go."

I decide to do as she suggests. I want to know more than anyone what the hell is going on. Depending on what I find out, I might not be willing to share it with everyone, but I need to know for my own peace of mind. I nod and take my apron off.

"I'll be as quick as I can." I head outside and move towards the side of the building. It feels like ages have passed since Matt stormed out, but it's been no more than fifteen minutes. As I approach the corner, I hear Matt's voice. I stop walking, listening to what he's saying. It feels wrong, but he's not exactly open with me about anything, and if this is the way I have to find out exactly who Matt really is and what his agenda here is, then so be it.

I am fed up of my head buzzing with possibilities and of hearing the whispered thoughts of my colleagues when they think I can't hear them. Whatever is going on, it's clear to me that they all think I know something.

"Yes, I realize that," I hear Matt say. He sounds agitated rather than angry, like he's frustrated. "I know that too."

He goes quiet for a moment. "Yeah I get it. I fucked up big time. But in a way the problem is solved isn't it? I know it's not really the outcome we wanted, but the problem will go away now."

I cock my head at the words. *What problem? What resolution?*

"For what it's worth, I am actually sorry, but it's done now and dwelling on it and beating myself up over it isn't going to fix it is it? I will find a way to sort the mess out and make sure everything gets smoothed over."

He pauses again. "I — God dammit!" he shouts.

I hear a loud bang and I finally step around the corner. Matt's phone is away and he's cradling one hand in the other. His knuckles are grazed and bleeding and I work out what happened. Whoever he was arguing with on the phone clearly hung up, and Matt, in frustration punched the wall. I'm no closer to knowing what's going on, but it's obvious Matt has screwed up something big.

"You know the wall always wins right?" I say, nodding towards his hand as I reach out to take a look.

He pulls his hand back from me. "It's fine," he snaps.

I glance up at him, shocked at how he replied to me.

He shakes his head and runs his undamaged hand over his face. "I'm sorry. I didn't mean to snap at you. You're right, punching the wall was stupid. I just have a lot on my plate right now."

I shrug off his apology. "It's fine," I say. "What's going on Matt. What happened back there?"

He shakes his head. "Marco stepped over the line and he's paid for it," he says.

That doesn't even begin to answer my question and Matt must know it. I can feel myself getting angry. "Did you blackmail him?" I ask.

"Blackmail him? What are you talking about?" He looks genuinely confused.

"You showed him something and he just agreed to leave. I mean you're a waiter Matt and he was the manager. You have to have something on him or he would have fired you on the spot the way you were yelling and swearing at him."

"It sounds like you're taking his side," Matt accuses me.

"I'm not taking anyone's side." I sigh. "How can I when I don't even know what's going on? What do you have on him? And why were you so pissed that he fired James?"

"I didn't blackmail him Callie, jeez." That's all he says. No explanation for what he did and no explanation for why James is suddenly his chief concern.

"For fuck sake, Matt!" I shout, getting angry now. "Will you stop avoiding the question and just tell me what the hell is going on here, because it's clear to me that you're not who you say you are."

"Go back inside Callie," he says quietly.

"That's your answer? Go back inside? Or what Matt? Will you fire me too?"

"You're being dramatic," Matt says. "I don't know what you think is happening here, but whatever it is, I can pretty much guarantee it's not as bad as you're imagining it to be."

"So tell me what it is then!" I shout.

He slams his palm against the wall and makes a groaning sound deep in the back of his throat. He shakes his head and looks at me.

I can see the anger in his eyes.

"Look, just go back to work. I can't do this right now. I have to sort this shit out, and then we'll talk." He starts to walk away from me.

I feel my anger bubbling up inside of me. "If you walk away from me now Matt, then you walk away from me for good!" I shout.

He keeps walking, not even looking back. I feel like punching the wall myself, but I stop myself. Instead, I lean back on it, tipping my head back and sighing. I knew when I delivered the ultimatum that he might call my bluff. I hoped he wouldn't, but I knew there was a chance of it. Now he has, I wish I could take it back, but I can't.

It doesn't matter that I feel more alone than I have ever felt in my life. It doesn't matter that I feel like I might be letting the love of my life walk away from me. It doesn't matter how I feel about Matt, because the truth is, I don't know him. Not the real him. I know the image he's chosen to project, the lies he's filled me with.

I bite my lip, forcing the tears that threaten to spill down my face back inside. I can't cry here. I won't cry here. I won't cry at all for Matt. He's betrayed me, lied to me. And he doesn't even trust me enough to explain.

Fuck him.

I know by the way I feel empty inside that my feelings for Matt are very real, serious feelings, the kind that make me think we were starting something special. But I can't be with someone who hides things from me.

I push myself off the wall and head back to the restaurant. I never should have allowed myself to break my no dating colleagues rule, because boy... did this just get messy. And now I will have to face the barrage of questions from my friends inside, with no real answers for them.

How can I expect them to believe that I don't know any more than they do about who Matt is and why he's here, let alone how he got Marco to agree to resign?

Chapter Twenty

CALLIE

I am so relieved when my shift finally ends and I can just be alone with my thoughts for a while. Except as I head for the station to catch my train, I find that my mind is working overtime, and I realize that I don't really want to be alone with my thoughts – I just wanted to be out from that place with the side eyes and the whispering.

I pull my phone out of my pocket and scroll through my contacts until I find Chloe's name. I hit call and bring the phone up to my ear. Chloe answers the call in seconds.

"Can you talk?" I ask.

"Sure," Chloe says. "What's up?"

"Everything," I say. "And honestly Chloe, I'm not even being dramatic."

I tell her everything. About Matt and what happened with Marco and how the other wait staff reacted to me. I can picture Chloe shaking her head when I am done and she breathes out audibly, a half whistle.

"Wow. You really do work with some nasty bitches don't you?" she says.

I shrug my shoulders although I am aware that she can't see me.

"I don't know. I mean would you believe I didn't know anything if you were them?" I say. The silence from the other end of the line tells me everything I need to know about that one. "See. It's not them in the wrong really. It's Matt. I feel like I have no idea who he really is."

"So ask him," Chloe says. She makes it sound so simple. "Call him and ask him what's going on."

"I asked him once already and he as good as told me to mind my own business. He had his chance," I say.

"So then you'll never know and you might just throw away Mr Right because you're so damned stubborn," Chloe says.

"Seriously, you're meant to be on my side. I called you so you could call Matt all of the bastards under the sun and tell me I'm better off without him," I say, half laughing.

"Well if it turns out he really is some shady gangster type who is into who knows what, then I'll say all of that. And if he turns out not to be, then I'll say I told you so instead," Chloe says. "I mean you said it yourself Callie – there's nothing he could have said that would have made you walk away from him."

"But that's the thing isn't it? He didn't say anything. I can handle difficult truths. What I can't handle is secrets and lies," I point out.

"Right," Chloe says. "Then tell Matt that. Give him a second chance Cal."

I open my mouth to tell her that I can't do that, that it's too late, but she gets in before I can interrupt.

"And before you say it's too late and you can't do it, promise me you'll at least think about it," she says.

"Fine," I say, feeling my mouth spreading into a genuine smile for probably the first time today. "I promise."

"Good," Chloe says. "Now go home and eat ice cream and drink wine and watch some crappy feel good rom coms."

I agree to this, although I'm not sure I am quite ready to become Bridget Jones just yet.

Chapter Twenty-One

CALLIE

I go to work the next day with a feeling of dread lodged in my stomach that makes me feel sick.

I spent the rest of yesterday's shift fielding questions and biting back tears. I honestly don't know how I kept my cool as everyone fucking quizzed me, but somehow, I did. By the end of the shift, I felt emotionally drained, empty inside except for this ball of hurt and anger.

I was angry at Matt for lying to me, betraying me, leading me on, and then walking away from me. And I was angry at him for leaving me in a situation where none of my friends really believed I didn't have any more of an idea about what was going on than they did. And the worst part? It occurred to me that there was really no explanation Matt could have given me that would have pushed me away instead of having me stand by.

I mean if he was blackmailing Marco, then he could only do that if Marco had done something bad enough he needed to keep it a secret, and I couldn't say he didn't deserve to lose his job after the way he treated me, and for firing James, which I did manage to find out was all because James had come to work ten minutes late.

Instead, Matt had walked away from me, leaving me heart broken and angry. Well, he had made his choice and I was done letting him take up space in my head. My life had been just fine before he came along, and while I couldn't deny being with him had made it better, I knew it would be just fine again.

None of that stopped the dread from sitting in a tight ball in my stomach as I hung my coat up in the break room. Another reason for my rule of not dating a coworker. I would have to face Matt at work. Would have to close up with him, just the two of us. That would be awkward to say the least.

I take a deep breath and walk out of the break room with my head held high. I'm not the one who has caused this between us, and I'm damned if I'm going to be the one who feels like they have to hide away.

As I step into the corridor, I see a man in a suit walking along it towards me. "Excuse me, sir?" I say. "The customer restrooms are back that way. I can show you."

The man smiles at me. "That's good to know. Callie, right?"

I nod, wondering how the customer knows my name. And why he's still coming towards me, instead of turning around. I guess it's going to be one of those nights.

The customer reaches me and holds out his hand. "Stewart Gillespie. I'm the new manager," he says with a warm smile.

"Oh," I say, taking his hand and shaking it. "I'm so sorry, I had no idea you would be starting today."

"Don't worry about it. I didn't know myself until a couple of hours ago. I was originally employed for a different restaurant, but well, here I am," he says, returning my smile.

Already I like him better than I ever liked Marco. His smile seems warm but professional, and I don't feel like he's trying to undress me with his eyes.

"I was told you're the shift supervisor here and that you could show me the ropes," he says. "Obviously, I know how the whole manager thing works. I've been doing it for long enough. But if you could just walk me through the staff, who's who, the hours they work, that kind of thing, I would really appreciate it."

So Marco did file the paperwork. I haven't lost my promotion. At least something good has come out of this. "Sure," I say, glad to have an excuse not to immediately go to the dining room and have to face Matt.

I follow him along the corridor and into the office that was Marco's and is now his. I am dying to ask him if he knows what went down with Marco, but I decide it's extremely unprofessional, and I bite my tongue about the whole situation. "So did you get the short straw then?" I ask. "Coming here instead of the other branch?"

"Actually no." He grins. "This place is within walking distance of my apartment. The other branch was a forty-minute drive each way. And just between me and you, this place is a hell of a lot nicer than the other place."

I spend the next hour or so filling Stewart in on the details of the restaurant. I tell him who can work which shifts, how many staff we usually have in place for each shift, and all of the little things that don't seem important until you've worked in the trade long enough to know they're often the most important things. I am careful to avoid any gossip or telling him too much.

"Thank you, Callie," he says when I've finished. "You've been very helpful. Now I think I've taken up enough of your time, so I'll let you go on."

"No worries." I leave the office satisfied I've done a good job of getting him up to speed. I head out into the dining area and ask Harriet which section is busiest, so I know where to place myself.

She shrugs and turns away from me.

I frown, but I dismiss it as I see her loaded up with four plates. She's obviously just busy. I take a moment to assess the floor and work out for myself where I will be the most useful.

"Stewart seems nice doesn't he?" I comment to Sasha as we pass each other on the floor.

"Wonderful." She keeps going, not pausing to chat. It's unlike her, but I guess it's the effect of having a new manager. No one wants to be the one caught standing around chatting first.

I've been on the restaurant floor around half an hour when the restaurant starts to quiet down. I haven't seen Matt yet and I'm starting to relax. He's obviously not coming in tonight for whatever reason. I try to start a conversation with Mark, one of the waiters, but he brushes me off. I walk away, wondering what the hell is going on. It's starting to seem like there's more to this than just not wanting to be caught chatting.

I decide I'm being paranoid. The whole Matt thing has got me looking for problems where there aren't any now. I go to the cleaning cupboard and get out the glass spray and a cloth.

It's a little too quiet for all of the wait staff to be kept busy, so I might as well do something useful. I move to the front of the dining room and begin polishing up the large windows that make up the front of the restaurant.

I'm halfway through the first one when Stewart appears beside me. I hope he's not one of those managers who thinks we can't do any sort of cleaning when there are diners in, and then expects us to stay for ages after our shifts end to clean up.

"You don't have to do that on my account." He smiles.

I laugh a little, relaxing. It doesn't sound like he's here to tell me not to do the cleaning around the diners. "I'd rather be busy. And when it quiets down like this, the shift supervisor is always the one to drop back from waiting on customers as we get paid a little more than the others, so it seems only fair that they're first in line to get the tips."

"Fair enough." He nods. "Makes sense." He walks away from me and walks around the floor for a while, chatting to the staff and some of the customers.

I finish the first of the windows and move on to the second one.

Sasha approaches me as I'm finishing it. "It's really dying down now. Do you mind if I go for my break?"

I cast a quick look around the dining room. She's right. There are only three full tables in the whole place. "No that's fine," I say. "Hang on a second and I'll come with you." I'm sure I see her roll her eyes, but I'm not quite sure enough to ask her about it. I go over to Harriet and tell her Sasha and I are going on our break and to give me a yell if they start getting busier.

She nods, but doesn't say anything.

I let it go, turning back to nod at Sasha that I'm ready, but she's already gone.

I know now I'm not imagining any of this. All of the wait staff are being off with me. Even the chef who I usually get on with really well has been kind of distant with me. In fact, the only person who's been remotely nice to me today is Stewart. I head out to the back and down to the break room. I'm going to quiz Sasha and find out what the hell is going on, and why I'm suddenly public enemy number one. Surely, this isn't because of yesterday? I mean none of the staff liked Marco anyway.

I go to the break room, ready to find out what's going on. Sasha barely glances at me as I walk in and I can't help but notice that she's made herself a coffee and not made one for me.

I make myself a drink and then I sit down. "What's going on?" I ask.

Sasha shrugs.

"Oh, come on Sash, don't give me that shit. I know everyone's pissed with me, I just need to know what I'm supposed to have done."

"It would be easier if you stopped pretending like you don't know what happened," she says.

I frown. So this is about yesterday. "Is this about Marco? I have no idea what happened there."

"It's not so much Marco. He deserved to go. It's more the fact we were all under suspicion and you didn't say a thing."

"Sasha I have no idea what you're talking about," I say.

Sasha reaches into her apron pocket and pulls out her phone. She looks at the screen and presses it a few times.

I start to think our conversation is done and this is her way of ignoring me.

She throws her phone down on the table in front of me. "Everyone knows. You can stop pretending now."

I frown, but I pick up the phone. I glance over the headline. Something about a family run business empire that's donated a load of money to some charity. *What the hell does this have to do with me?* I reread the headline, and that's when the name jumps out at me. Hunter. But it can't be anything to do with Matt. I mean he's a waiter, not a business empire owner.

I scroll down, and a photograph of three smiling young men appears. There, smack bang in the middle is Matt. He's a little younger in the picture, but there's no mistaking it's him.

I push the phone back to Sasha, my mind reeling.

She doesn't seem to notice my complete amazement. Instead, she starts to explain, "When I came to work this morning on the opening shift, Stewart was here. He brought us all in here and explained it all. Matt's no fucking waiter. His family owns the restaurant chain. And half of the businesses in the city by the looks of it. He's old money, a billionaire. But you knew that didn't you? Did you know him before he even came here?"

"I — no," I stutter, still trying to process what she's telling me.

"His whole thing here was a ruse. He pretended to be a waiter so he could infiltrate the business. There was money going missing and he wanted to find out who it was. I guess it was Marco."

"So let me get this straight. Marco steals off the business, and everyone is somehow pissed at me that he gets fired for it, even though you all hate him?"

"No Callie, everyone is pissed at you because you went along with it and didn't say a word to anyone. We're meant to be your friends and we were all under suspicion at one point. And you didn't say a fucking thing. I'm not surprised you got promoted. Fucking the boss is a good way up the ladder isn't it?"

"I didn't know Sash," I say, begging her with my eyes to believe me.

She won't even look at me. She just shakes her head and stands up. "Drop the lies Callie," she says as she storms out.

I sit alone in the silence, my mind reeling. It all makes sense all of a sudden. Matt's quiet arrogance when he first started, how he always seemed to have more money than the rest of us put together. How he got away with speaking to Marco the way he did.

And the card he showed Marco. It wasn't a bribe. He was showing him his true identity. That's why Marco agreed to leave without a fuss. He knew Matt knew what he was up to and he chose to leave while he still could.

It explains why I got promoted as well. I might not have known I was fucking the boss, but I was. And a couple of days after me telling Matt I was paying my way through college with this job, a promotion and a pay rise lands in my lap.

How could I have been so naïve? How could I not have seen it?

I was so caught up in the romance, in Matt, that I missed all of the signs. It also explains why Stewart was nice to me. He thinks I'm the owner's girlfriend. And it explains why he didn't feel the need to tell me any of this when he has told all of the other staff. He assumed I would know.

I can feel tears prickling my eyes again. I have fallen for Matt, far deeper than I care to admit. And the whole thing has been nothing but a game to him. A ruse. He was using me, getting close to me, hoping I knew something. That's why he never told me anything about himself. That's why he never took me to his apartment. He didn't want me to know who he really was. Because then it would have been game over. Did he suspect me? Was he trying to catch me by taking me to expensive places to see if I had the money to pay for that kind of shit?

A single tear runs down my face as the truth comes crashing down around me. Matt used me. And now, he's found out who was ripping him off and he's gone, leaving me behind — without so much as a goodbye and thanks for all the sex.

I stand up abruptly, almost knocking my chair over. I have put up with so much shit working here because I need the money, but I don't need it enough to stay here now. Not after this. I can't work somewhere where everyone is gossiping about me, about the girl who slept her way up the ladder.

I grab my jacket and my handbag then go to Stewart's office. I don't bother to knock.

Stewart looks annoyed when he glances up, but his expression turns to concern when he sees me.

It's then, I realize tears are running down my face. I wipe them away angrily. "I quit," I say and then I turn around.

Stewart jumps to his feet. "Callie, wait. What's going on? What happened?" he asks.

"I just found out the last few weeks of my life have been a lie. And I can't stay working here. Did Matt tell you to be nice to me?"

"Who the hell is Matt?" Stewart asks.

"The owner," I say, surprised that he doesn't seem to know what I mean.

"I've never met the owner. My interview was carried out by Janine at HR and all of my paperwork and checks have gone through her. Callie, please sit down and let's try and work this out," he pleads.

Ok, I was wrong about Stewart. He was nice to me because it's his style to be nice to his employees obviously. But it doesn't change anything else. It doesn't make me feel any less betrayed. I feel used, dirty, and being here is going to be a constant reminder for me. I shake my head. "I'm sorry to leave you in the lurch like this, but I can't stay. This is beyond the point where it can be worked out. Sasha has worked here as long as I have. She can step up and be shift supervisor."

I walk away before he can say anything else. I am just about managing to bite back the tears now, and if he says anything nice to me, I'm afraid it'll be like a flood gate opening, and I want to walk out of here with my head held high, with what little dignity I have left still intact.

I decide to leave through the dining room. I want them all to see me, to see they haven't broken me. Maybe to even realize they judged me with no idea what was actually going on. Because if they feel betrayed, it's not even close to how I feel.

"Callie? Where are you going?" Sasha asks as I step into the dining room.

"I've quit... I had no idea Matt was the owner and trust me, I feel more betrayed than anyone here. But you know what Sash? A stranger betrayed you. And yes, me as well, because clearly I never knew the real Matt. But that's not what hurts. What hurts is knowing everyone here, people who I thought of as friends, all assumed I would go behind their backs this way, and not one person, not even you, thought to come to me about it."

"Callie, wait..." Sasha says as I walk away,

"There's nothing to wait for." I ignore her calling my name as I walk to the door. I pull it open and step out into the night. I wait until I'm out of sight of the restaurant before I let the tears fall once more.

Matt has well and truly played me for a fool. I actually believed him when he told me he cared about me. That I was his. I have to give him his dues. He faked being into me extremely well. But now I see it. He has broken my heart and now he's taken away my job too. He really did a fucking number on me, and if I hear the name Matthew Hunter again in this life time, it'll be too fucking soon.

Chapter Twenty-Two

CALLIE

The morning after I quit my job started out like any other morning. I got up, showered, and got ready. It wasn't until I was grabbing my handbag and heading out of my dorm room I realized I now had no way to pay the bills. I was covered until the end of this month, and my final paycheck would cover next month, but after that, I was screwed with a capital S.

It meant I had around six weeks to find another job. There were plenty of other restaurants around, and with my experience, in theory, I could walk into any one of them, but who was I going to get a reference from? Marco? Yeah, right. He wouldn't have done me any favors even before Matt fired him. Stewart? He seemed like a nice guy, but he didn't know anything about me so he could hardly vouch for my work ethic or skills. Matt? *Ha, there's a joke.*

I told myself to stop being so dramatic. I could always contact HR and get a standard company reference. Surely it would be enough to get a job? If all else failed, I'd have to find something else. Maybe I could see one of my professors and ask about doing some TA work, something I'd always tried to avoid because TAs worked an insane amount of hours and I didn't want anything that would encroach on my studies. I wasn't going to get myself into a financial mess to then fail my classes because I didn't have the time to study.

I walk briskly, trying to outrun my thoughts. When my head wasn't spinning with what the fuck I was meant to do for a job, it was filled with Matt. How he could have lied to me about who he really was all of this time? How he had turned all of my friends at the restaurant against me? It didn't even matter that the latter part wasn't directly his fault. It was all a part of the same thing. If he had told me the truth, I never would have blabbed to the others, but at least then I'd have been ostracized for something I had actually done. And I never would have taken the promotion.

I could see why they didn't believe me when I told them I didn't know the truth about Matt's identity though. I mean who would believe that someone didn't really know who their boyfriend was? If this had been the other way around and I wasn't involved, I'd have either thought the girl was lying, or that she was incredibly stupid and naïve.

So yeah, that's me. Stupid and naïve.

I scream inside of my head, telling my thoughts to just quit it, and for a moment they do, allowing me to focus on my plans for the day. I'm on my way to the library now to finish up a paper that's due tomorrow. And then I have a couple of hours before my lecture, time I'm going to use job hunting. Maybe I'll ask in the library, see if they need anyone.

As my head starts to clear and I am once more taking in my surroundings, I notice an all black car with blacked out windows moving along the road beside me. There's nothing particularly alarming about the car. It looks like the sort of car a well to do lawyer gets driven around in, but the way it's moving so slowly, like it's tailing me, alarms me.

I tell myself I'm being paranoid, that the driver is clearly looking for an address. I need to be sure though. I stop walking and dig through my handbag, pretending I'm looking for something. Sure enough, the black car pulls into the curb behind me. Scared now, I begin to walk again, much faster than I was previously walking.

I scan to my left and my right, looking for a shop or a bar or something. Anywhere I can duck into. There's nothing. All of the buildings on this street are residential, and I'm not about to barge into someone's home with a story about how I may or may not have been being followed. I am being followed though. I'm almost certain of it.

My heart is slamming in my chest. I up my pace again, moving so fast now that I'm almost running. I keep my gaze straight ahead, trying not to look at the car. I'm just pleased there are a few other people walking along the street, other-wise, who knows what might happen.

I hear rather than see the window of the car going down, a smooth, electronic whirring sound that I never would have noticed if my senses weren't suddenly hyper aware of the car.

"Callie," I hear.

Fuck. I'm definitely not being paranoid. Whoever is in that car knows my name. I keep walking, my eyes darting around, looking for a way out of the street.

"Callie," I hear again.

It dawns on me that I recognize the voice and I glance back over my shoulder, already knowing it's him. *Matt.* I am right.

He's half hanging out of the window, calling after me. Looking at him now, even after everything, I can't help but feel a wave of desire rushing through my body, but I ignore it.

I shake my head, roll my eyes and turn away from Matt. I keep walking in the direction I was heading in, although I no longer almost run. Matt might be a lot of things I don't want to think about, but he's hardly going to drag me into a car and abduct me.

I hear the car engine stop and the door open and then close. I hear footsteps behind me, running to catch up with me. "Callie, wait," Matt shouts.

God, the guy really can't take a hint can he? I feel a hand on my shoulder, turning me. I stop abruptly and turn to face Matt. I ignore the desire I feel, concentrating instead on the anger bubbling up inside of myself. "Are you fucking insane? Who follows someone like that in a car with blacked out windows?" I shout, focusing on the lesser of the evils he's committed.

"I — I'm sorry," he says. "I didn't mean to scare you. I was just trying to get up the courage to talk to you."

"Stop following me Matt," I snap. "I don't want to see you and I certainly don't want to talk. I have nothing to say to you."

He looks hurt and I feel a rush of guilt before I remind myself that our whole relationship was a lie. If anyone should be wearing that hurt puppy look, it's me. I turn away from Matt again, but he grabs my hand and holds it in his. It's obvious he's not ready to let me walk away from him, so I decide to hear him out and then he'll have no reason to keep on following me. "What do you want?" I demand.

"I heard you quit your job. I just wanted to make sure you're okay."

I snort out a bitter laugh. "I'm just peachy. Now if that's it...?"

He still holds my hand in his and I have to fight to not let myself feel the sparks where our hands touch. Matt might have only pretended to have feelings for me, but the lust? That's real.

"Why did you leave the restaurant?" he asks.

Seriously? I thought I was slow on the uptake. How can he not see what's going on here? "Let me see. Maybe because everyone at work thinks I was in on your little ruse. And that I betrayed all of their trust."

"Shit," Matt says. "I'm sorry, Callie. I didn't think of that. Look I can fix this."

"That's not even the worst part," I say, before I can stop myself.

Dammit. I had no intention of saying more, but I have to now since I've led in with that.

Matt's looking at me questioningly, waiting for me to elaborate.

Oh screw it, I'll just tell him the truth. What does it matter now?

"You know when Marco came onto me, I didn't find him remotely attractive. But even if I had been attracted to him, I would never have slept with him. You know why? Because the idea of getting a promotion because I was fucking the boss turned my stomach. Days after I told you I was paying my own way through college, I mysteriously got a promotion and a pay rise. I wonder why that could be? Oh, yeah. Because I was fucking the boss."

"Callie no, it wasn't like that. Let me explain —"

"Save your explanation for someone who gives a shit Matt, because quite frankly, I'm done with you and I'm done with this conversation. Now if you'll excuse me, I have a class to get to."

It's a lie, but after Matt lied about literally everything, I feel it's justified. I try to pull my hand away, but Matt isn't letting go of me. I pull harder, but he only tightens his grip.

A man passing by pauses to look at us. "Are you alright, miss?" he asks.

"She's fine," Matt says.

The man ignores him, waiting for me to confirm I am indeed all right. I could say no, he won't let go of me, but I'm not about to instigate a fight. Instead, I nod and give what I hope is a sheepish smile. "I'm fine, thank you," I say. "Just a stupid argument." I glare pointedly at where Matt still holds onto me.

He releases me and the man keeps walking.

I start to walk away, hoping this will be the end of it. The longer I spend with Matt, the harder it's getting to stay so angry at him. I can feel myself starting to cave in, to at least want to hear how he thinks he can justify all of this.

It isn't the end of it. Matt closes the gap between us in two long strides.

I keep walking, not even looking at him, and he falls into step beside me. "Look I get why you're angry. Really I do. I would be too. And I know you don't owe me anything, but please let's just grab a coffee or something and let me explain."

"I've told you, I'm running late for class," I say.

"Okay. Dinner tonight then. We'll talk, and I swear I'll tell you anything you want to know. After that, if you never want to see me again, you have my word I'll leave you alone."

"Fine," I hear myself say before I have a chance to really think it through.

Curiosity has gotten the better of me. I have to have some answers so I can get closure and move on. At least that's what I tell myself, because it's an easier truth to swallow than the real truth. The truth where I want Matt to be able to explain things in a way that makes sense to me. In a way where I can forgive him.

Not that it matters. We're done. I was just a pawn in his James Bond game. He only wants to explain to ease his own conscience. I'm about to open my mouth to tell him I've changed my mind, and I don't want to hear it.

"I'll pick you up from your dorm room at seven. See you then," Matt says before I have a chance to speak.

"Whatever," I say, cursing inwardly that he got in before me and I lost my chance to change my mind.

"See you tonight." Matt turns and walks back towards the car which has been idling at the curb waiting for him.

I have to admit he's good. He sensed I was ready to call the whole thing off, so he got the hell away from me before I could tell him no. I could still text him and cancel, but we both know I won't do that. We both know I have way too many questions to back out of this now.

Chapter Twenty-Three

CALLIE

I wait nervously for Matt, pacing the floor of my dorm's entrance way. I am wearing a short black dress and high heels. I have no idea where Matt is planning on taking me, and I don't care. I haven't dressed up for him. I've done it to make myself feel confident. I don't want a repeat of the last time we went for a meal and I felt so out of place.

I check my phone for the time. It's only ten to seven. I keep pacing. I am so nervous I can taste the coppery adrenaline in my mouth. I tell myself to calm down. It's not like it matters what I say or do. Matt and I aren't a thing. We never were anyway except in my own head. I suddenly know tonight is going to be a disaster. At least today hasn't been a total write off.

I didn't get much of my paper done in the library, but I did manage to talk to the librarian about my job hunt and she told me about a part time position in the library which they usually like to fill with a student. I filled out an application form there and then and I had a good feeling about that. I love books and I let it show as I chatted to the librarian. I think she liked me too, which is a good start.

The door to my dorm opens and there he is, early. He's dressed in fashionable ripped jeans and a cream colored dress shirt. I get a whiff of his no doubt expensive aftershave as he spots me and steps closer to me.

He kisses my cheek before I can stop him and I try to ignore the tightening in my stomach as his lips touch my skin and I smell the scent of him beneath the aftershave. "Hi," I mutter.

"Hey," he says. "You ready?"

If he finds it strange that I'm in the lobby of the building instead of letting him up to my room like I usually do, he doesn't mention it. I nod tersely and he pulls the door open for me. I step through it, thanking him more out of habit than any real gratitude.

He leads me to a gleaming red Maserati and opens the door for me. I get in and he closes the door and hurries around to the driver's side. He gets in.

"Another one of your brother's cars, so you could impress the poor girl?" I ask sarcastically.

Matt looks at me and I can see the tension in his face.

I feel a pull of guilt which I ignore. He's brought this on himself.

"Actually it's mine. So was the other one. And I have another couple too. I would like to impress you Callie, but let's be honest. It's going to take more than a flashy car for me to make a good impression on you."

He's got that much right at least. I make a non-committal grunt.

Matt pulls away from the curb and we drive off. The car doesn't so much growl as it purrs. It's smooth, almost silent, and I have to admit that under any normal circumstances, I'd love this car.

That's the thing though isn't it? These aren't any normal circumstances. Normally, when Matt and I are together, the conversation flows easily and we end up laughing at something stupid, but tonight, there's no laughter. There's not even any conversation. There's just this awkward silence that hangs in the air, a physical thing, a barrier that I'm not sure we can ever break through.

It occurs to me that even if Matt manages to give me an explanation for all of the lies, one I can live with, we still can't be together. I don't fit into his world, and I refuse to be his project, the little poor girl he saves from her shitty life.

Whatever happens between Matt and me tonight, this will be the last time I see him. The notion sends a pang of regret through me, but it also eases some of my tension. I don't have anything to be nervous about. Nothing is riding on this. It's just my chance to get some answers before I forget about Matt altogether and get on with my life. "Why did you take the train every day if you have, what, four sports cars?" I ask.

"Five," Matt says.

I frown at this answer.

He smiles apologetically. "Sorry... but I did promise you total honesty. It's not four cars, it's five. I took the train that first day because I wanted to talk to you, to see if you could give me anything I could use. But after that? Honestly Callie, I did it because I wanted to get to know you better. I would rather have walked home through snow and rain with you than driven home without you."

Well, the first part of that is honest at least.

"Look Matt if we're going to do this, then you need to know that you don't have to try and make me feel better. I know I was just a piece of the puzzle to you, a game, and I can make my peace with that. So you don't need to try and make out that you actually wanted to be around me."

Matt laughs.

It's a sound that surprises me and I frown.

He shakes his head and glances at me before turning his eyes back to the road. "You're giving me much more credit as an actor than I deserve. You were never part of any sort of game."

His words should soothe me, but they don't. Instead, they put me on edge. Could it be possible? Could what we had have been real? I can't let myself go there. Instead, I focus on the questions swirling through my mind. I decide to start with the smaller ones, leading up to the real issues. I don't think I'm ready to ask the big questions yet. "When we went to that restaurant, you lied about knowing the owner didn't you? You just paid full price?"

"Yes and no," Matt says. "I paid full price because I chose to. I own the place."

"Oh..." I pause, taken aback once more.

That certainly explains why he was confident we wouldn't be turned away, and it explains why all of the staff were so familiar with him. It does give him a few brownie points though. None of the staff seemed nervous around him, and he treated them all with respect.

"Who was the man who interrupted us at the table to buy you a drink?" I ask.

"I still don't know," he says. "He never did call. I think he just recognized me and wanted to say hello."

"At least, he knew who you actually were, so he had one up on me I guess," I say bitterly.

Matt glances at me again, and then he pulls next to the curb.

I look around, but there's no sign of anywhere we could be eating here.

Matt turns to face me, the engine still running. "Listen to me Callie. If you only believe one thing I tell you today, then make sure it's this. I didn't tell you everything, and I should have. I see that now. But I have never lied about who I am. Everything you've seen of me has been the real me. The money, the power? They're just material things. They're not important. What's important is who I am as a person, and that hasn't changed."

"You're telling me that a billionaire businessman genuinely enjoyed drinking cheap wine from the bottle in the park?" I ask, raising an eyebrow.

"Yes. And I enjoyed watching you squirm in that cooking lesson doorway. And I enjoyed running through the rain with you and sharing popcorn with you. I even enjoyed the terrible college party. You know why? Because of you Callie. I would happily go and sit in a field in the middle of nowhere as long as you were with me." He doesn't wait for an answer, he just pulls back and starts driving again.

My head is swirling. He isn't acting any different from the Matt I knew. Ok, maybe he's a little awkward, but then so am I. He's not acting like he suddenly thinks he's better than me, or like I am nothing but a nuisance that needs to be shut up and made to go away.

I suddenly realize we're heading away from the city center and I frown slightly as I look out of the window. I don't recognize any of the buildings here. "Where are we going?" I ask.

"The one place I could think of that you might actually want to go," he replies. "My apartment. I'm going to cook you dinner and then we're going to talk for as long as it takes me to convince you to give me another chance."

I'm still not sure there's enough time in the world for that to happen, but I can't help but smile a little when he says he's taking me to his apartment. It'll be nice to finally see the place he's been keeping me away from since the moment we met. "It's a proper bachelor pad isn't it? Like a real dive. That's why you've always kept me away from it," I say, my tone light.

"Yeah, that's it. I'm a total slob. Pizza boxes all over, half empty cans of beer on every surface. But don't worry, I had my housekeeper take care of it all," he replies.

My head turns quickly to look at him. A housekeeper? I relax when I see the twinkle in his eyes.

"I'm just kidding Callie. As if I'd leave half of the beer."

Against my will, I feel myself laughing and the tension between us starts to fade a little.

*W*hen we pull up outside of a swanky looking apartment building, I'm pleased to note it is indeed in Felton. At least, he was honest about that much. He didn't mention the fact it's in the really expensive end, but then again, I never asked.

I don't wait for Matt to come and get my door. I get out of the car myself, looking at the building with its steel and glass entryway complete with an actual doorman.

A man appears, seemingly out of nowhere and Matt hands him his car keys. A doorman and a valet. I wonder if he was really joking about the housekeeper. He probably has a butler too.

Matt comes to my side and offers me his arm.

I debate not taking it, but I find myself slipping my arm through his. Fireworks sizzle in my stomach when we touch and my pussy clenches. Clearly, my body isn't on the same page as my mind on this one.

Matt leads me into the building, greeting the doorman on the way in. He leads me to the elevator. He presses the call button and the door pings open. The elevator is huge, mirrors on every wall. We step in and I look anywhere but at my own reflection.

Matt pulls a credit card sized card out of his pocket and pushes it into a slot. The button for the penthouse apartment lights up when the card goes in the slot and Matt presses it.

I swallow hard. I am so far out of my depth here.

The elevator moves upwards and I remember the last time I was in an elevator with Matt. We were in a hotel, going up to a room to celebrate my promotion. I wanted to jump on him in the elevator but we weren't alone. Now we are, and although my body still wants to jump on Matt, my head is in control, and it's giving me a resounding no.

Finally, the doors ping open and the moment passes. I step out of the elevator into a short hallway with only one door leading off it.

Matt steps around me and unlocks the door with the same card he used in the elevator. He pushes the door open and gestures for me to enter.

I go in and gasp when I see the place. The living room, dining area and kitchen are one huge open plan room, big enough for my childhood home to fit in and still have space left over. The wall opposite me is all glass, giving me a gorgeous view over the city. We're high enough up that even with the glass wall, the place feels private.

I take a step forward and then I slip my shoes off, conscious of my heels on the hardwood flooring. I move them to the side of the door and look around again. The kitchen area is immaculate, the countertops and appliances gleaming. There's a big mahogany table with eight chairs beside the giant window at the kitchen end. In the living room area, a big black leather couch takes center stage, a glass coffee table in front of it. On the wall, a huge TV.

Opposite the window is an aquarium, lit up, and full of fish of every color built into the wall. Bubbles float lazily up to the surface where they pop, each one giving off a tiny spray.

The whole apartment is decorated in muted creams and browns. Tasteful, masculine, yet far from a bachelor pad.

"It's beautiful," I breathe.

"Thanks," Matt says. "Although I can't take much credit for it to be honest. Give me a restaurant and I can design you a perfect dining area, but give me a home, and I'm lost. This is all Chance's design skills. He's the arty one."

"Your brother?" I say.

Matt nods.

"Yeah. Chance is the arty one, Seb is the numbers guy, and I'm the foodie. Everything I told you about my childhood was true. My mom really did instill a love for food in me. I guess that's why I was attracted to the restaurant side of the business. And now you know why I didn't train to be a chef. My dad would have never allowed it. Our paths were clear. Grow up and get involved in the business."

"You make it sound so normal. Like growing up a billionaire is nothing," I say.

Matt shrugs. "The thing is, to me it is normal. It's just the way it was. Come on, sit down. I'll pour us some wine and then put our dinner on. Are you hungry?"

I give him a small nod as I walk to the long counter that separates the kitchen area from the rest of the room. Tall stools run the length of it and I perch on one of the stools, watching Matt as he goes to the fridge and pulls out a bottle of rose wine.

"You did say you preferred rose right?" he says.

I can't help but smile as I nod. Maybe Matt lied about a lot, but it's becoming clear to me that while we were together, he did listen to me. I told him in the restaurant we went to that I would have ordered rose wine.

He pours two glasses and hands one to me. He pauses for a moment and then he lifts his glass. "To honesty," he says.

"I'll drink to that." I clink my glass against his.

He takes a drink from his own glass and then he moves around the kitchen, chopping, dicing, frying and doing all manner of clever things with chicken and vegetables.

"You really can cook then," I say.

"I like to think so, but you haven't tasted it yet," Matt smiles. "But don't worry. Whatever happens to our main course, I have dessert in the fridge, made by a world class pastry chef."

I go quiet, reminded once more of the difference between our lives. Matt and his world class dessert chef. Me and a cheese-cake bought from Kroger.

"You've gone quiet," Matt points out. "My mom would be really upset to think you weren't looking forward to her world famous Pavlova."

"Your mom made dessert?" I say.

Matt nods.

"Yup. She's by far the best dessert maker I've ever known. And I've known a lot of pastry chefs."

I pause at this. Maybe Matt and I aren't so different after all. I mean everyone thinks their mom's cooking is the best don't they? "Can I ask you something?"

"Anything," Matt says, serious suddenly.

"Where's your bathroom?" I finally smile.

Seeing I have mellowed a bit, he relaxes a little. "Through the living room, down the hall, the last door on the right," he says.

I hop off the stool and follow his directions. It's exactly as I pictured it. Black granite surfaces that gleam, a huge claw-footed bathtub, a shower that looks big enough to hold a football team, and a quite impressive array of lotions and potions. I do my business and wash my hands and then I go back to my perch. "You have quite an impressive collection of toiletries," I grin. "How long does it take you to get ready in the morning?"

"I just roll out of bed, looking this good." Matt winks. "They're just decoration."

I almost smile then choose to roll my eyes. It's starting to feel normal between Matt and me. Too normal. Like we haven't got this giant weight hanging over our heads. Maybe I should forget all of my questions and just enjoy a civilized goodbye dinner with Matt, but I know I'll regret it if I don't get the answers I need.

"It's almost ready. Why don't you go take a seat at the table?" Matt says.

I get off the stool and swallow down the rest of my wine, enjoying the warm feeling in my stomach. I want to be just tipsy enough to be brave and ask everything I want to ask. But I don't want to be drunk.

Matt tops off my glass before I go to the table and then he hands me the bottle. "Might as well take it to the table," he says. "You're probably going to need it."

"Why?" I ask, suspicious suddenly.

"Well you're about to eat my home cooked food aren't you?" Matt grins.

I take my glass and the bottle and choose a seat that gives me a view of the city. Dusk is starting to fall and lights are coming on. "This really is a spectacular view. How do you get anything done here?" I ask over my shoulder.

Matt comes towards the table with his glass. He tops it off and places it down opposite me. "My home office is on the other side of the apartment," he says. "When I first moved in here, I had this idea in my head of sitting right where you are now on my laptop. But of course it didn't happen. I was far too nosey."

He heads back to the kitchen and returns with two plates. He puts one down in front of me and takes his seat. "Bone apple tea." He grins.

I crack a smile and shake my head. The meal looks wonderful. Chicken, mushrooms and spring onions mixed in a spicy smelling sauce with pasta. I take a forkful and chew it. "It's delicious."

Matt's smile tells me he knew this for a fact. He might have joked about his cooking, but he really does know his way around a kitchen.

I watch him subtly as he takes a forkful of his meal. He's still Matt. Still the man I was rapidly falling in love with. Isn't he? The money, the power, the wealthy family. It's a lot to get my head around, and even without trying to get to the bottom of Matt's lies, I'm feeling kind of overwhelmed by it all, like I've stepped into someone else's life.

I decide it's time to get to the bottom of everything. And then at least I can walk away knowing the truth. Or not. Who knows? I sure as hell don't anymore. "So, the restaurant... what made you do the whole undercover thing?"

"I told you. I'm a spy," Matt smiles. His face turns serious when he sees I'm not joking around anymore. "Where do I start?"

"The beginning." I might not like what I'm about to hear, but at least I know it will be true.

He nods and as he starts to speak, he gets this faraway look on his face, an expression that tells me he's genuinely remembering something rather than feeding me another pack of lies, "I've always been drawn to the restaurant side of the business for obvious reasons," Matt says. "But like I said earlier, Seb is the numbers guy, so it was actually him who spotted an anomaly in the books for La Trattoria. He came to me and told me he suspected something strange was going on with the finances. He brought in a professional auditor who confirmed that something was amiss. But at that point, we had no real proof there was anything but an incompetent manager in place. We had grounds to fire him, but we discussed it, and we decided we needed more information.

For starters, we needed to know if anyone else within the restaurant was in on the scheme if indeed there was a scheme. Seb suggested sending someone in to pose as a waiter and I said I would do it. My father wasn't overly happy about that idea, but I stood my ground. That restaurant is my baby, and I felt like I needed to handle it personally."

"So you told Marco you had been a manager of another branch?" I asked.

He shook his head. "No. He was just told I was transferring from another branch. The manager thing was just a rumor, but I let it go, because Marco seemed more open to talking to me about the goings on of the business when he thought I had been a manager. The plan was to catch Marco red handed and have him prosecuted, and as I said, work out if anyone else was in on his little money laundering scheme. It would have worked too, but then I met you and the whole thing went to shit," he says with a smile.

I raise an eyebrow. "You thought I was involved?"

Matt shakes his head, laughing. "No. That's not what I meant at all. It went to shit because once I met you, it compromised me. I could no longer be rational about it, keep the emotion out of it. When it was only money, it was easy to stay rational, cozy up to Marco, get him to trust me. But then I saw the way he treated you and when you told me he had hit on you, I just saw red. I couldn't keep the emotion out of it after that, and I found it increasingly difficult to even pretend to be friends with Marco. I should have pulled out at that point, but Marco might have gotten suspicious if I was replaced and the next guy, also tried to buddy up to him. I fought my instincts every time I saw that creep. But then he fired James. He claimed it was because he was late, which is a shitty enough reason, but that wasn't true. James had let something slip, something he had seen Marco do that struck him as odd. I don't know how Marco found out it was James who had told me where to look for concrete evidence of his crimes, but he knew."

"And James paid the price," I comment.

"Actually, he didn't. He has been given his job back with a nice fat cash bonus as a thank you for helping us weed out Marco."

"Oh," I say, surprised.

Matt smiles. "I know you think having money makes someone a monster Callie, but I don't use people as collateral damage."

"I didn't say that."

"You didn't have to," Matt says. "I can see how you're different around me. How talking about money makes you uncomfortable."

"It's just... you're from a different world."

"You'd be surprised," Matt says. "I'll admit, we had a nice house when I was growing up. Nice cars. I went to a private school. But believe it or not, I was never spoilt. My parents had a healthy attitude about money, and from a young age, they taught us that money can certainly make you comfortable, but it can't buy you happiness. They also taught us that we have to earn money, not just have it handed to us. Do you know how much allowance I got as a kid?"

I shake my head, waiting for a number that Matt thinks is low and I will think is absurdly high.

"Ten dollars a week," he says. "And to get that, I had to wash my dad's cars."

"Ok, I admit it. You have shocked me... I got the same amount, and I didn't have to do anything for it."

"See. Now who's the spoilt one?" Matt teases me as he gets up suddenly.

I frown.

"More wine," he says.

I didn't even realize it but I've drank another glass. I should slow down, maybe switch to water, but I don't object when Matt refills my glass. "So what happened to Marco then? You gave him the choice to leave quietly," I say.

"Yes. After I learned about what had happened to James, it was the final straw. I had held myself in check because I knew my personal feelings about you and the way Marco treated you were clouding my judgement, but when I felt the same way about the way he treated James, I don't know. I lost control. I revealed my identity too soon, and the whole thing was a bust. I mean we got rid of Marco, but we lost the chance to prosecute him. My father is not impressed in the least. And it doesn't help that Seb keeps bringing it up and tormenting me over it."

"No, I don't suppose it would," I say.

I know what's coming. The most important question. But suddenly, I don't want to ask it, because I am afraid of the answer. Instead, I ask a question I know I will like the answer to. "How about some of this famous Pavlova then?" I suggest.

"Are you sure you're ready for it? I mean after eating this, no dessert will ever fully satisfy you again," Matt warns.

"I'll take my chances." I nod.

Matt goes back to the kitchen.

I turn in my chair so I can watch him as he moves around the kitchen. He looks so at home there, so relaxed.

He cuts off two chunks of Pavlova and adds a squirt of cream and some berries to each plate. Finally, he drizzles the whole thing with what I think is raspberry coulis. He comes back to the table.

I turn back around, noting Matt's grin when he realizes I've been watching him. At least, he doesn't know I was appreciating the view, and he certainly doesn't know that my pussy is wet beneath the table.

"Ta-da," he says, putting a plate down in front of me with a flourish.

I pick up my spoon and try the Pavlova. "Ok, you win. It's definitely the best Pavlova I've ever tasted," I say.

He smiles as he sits down and starts on his own. We eat the dessert in silence, a comfortable enough silence, although there is still a slight tension in the air. Not enough to stop me from appreciating the creamy, crispy goodness of the Pavlova though. I finish the last bite and put my spoon down.

"Would you like some more?" Matt asks as he finishes his own.

"It was lovely, but I couldn't eat another thing. I'm so stuffed," I say.

He nods. He looks down at the table for a moment, fiddling with his spoon. Finally, he looks up at me, his face serious. "So what you really want to know is why I kept all of this from you isn't it? But you're holding back from asking because you're afraid I'll tell you something along the lines of it being none of your business and I couldn't give a shit if you got hurt."

"It's that obvious huh?" I try and fail to smile.

"I promised you honesty, so that's what you'll get," he says. "In the beginning, I couldn't tell you what was going on. I couldn't tell anyone. I had no idea who I could trust. It became clear to me very early on that you hated Marco, so you were never under any suspicion if that's what you're worried about."

It's not, but I don't tell Matt that. Because then I'll have to admit that what I'm really worried about is how hard I have fallen for someone who was playing a game with me.

"I wanted to tell you the truth. I almost did so many times. But I couldn't."

"Because it would have ruined your investigation?"

"No. I knew I could trust you not to say anything to anyone."

"So why then?" I prompt.

"Because I was terrified that what happened would happen," he says, not meeting my eye.

"I don't understand," I say.

He looks back up and his eyes hold mine.

I can feel the familiar stirring in my stomach, the throbbing of need in my clit. I blink and try to look away, but I can't tear my gaze from his.

"I was terrified you'd run a mile and I would lose you," he says.

"How could you lose something you never had?" I say. "What we had wasn't real Matt. It was all a lie."

He reaches over the table and takes my hand in his. "No. It wasn't. That first night when I caught the train with you, I admit I did it to see if you would say anything I could use. But after that? It was all real. I fell for you Callie, and everything that happened between us, that was all real too."

I want to believe him. I really do. But how can I? How can I believe anything he says now? The silence stretches out between us. He's clearly waiting for me to say something, but I don't know what to say.

"Callie? Say something. Please," he pleads.

"I — I don't know what to say," I admit.

He pulls his hand away from mine.

I have to fight to stop myself from reaching out and grabbing his hand, stopping him from releasing me from his grip.

He stands up and goes to the window, standing looking out at the city, his back to me. "I understand this is a lot to take in. I really am sorry for the mess I caused. If you can't decide yet whether or not to give me a second chance, how about you give the restaurant a second chance for now? I've spoken to HR and your job is there if you still want it."

"I don't," I say. "Like I told you earlier, I refuse to work somewhere where I get a promotion because I'm fucking the boss."

He turns back to me and I see a flash of anger in his eyes. "It's not like that Callie. Not on either count. Firstly, I had nothing to do with your promotion. I tried to explain that to you earlier. I didn't even know you were getting a promotion until you told me that night. Marco had it all worked out with HR. You got that promotion because you deserved it."

That is perhaps the biggest surprise of the night so far. Marco actually played fair and gave me a promotion I deserved based on my work.

Before I can respond, Matt goes on, "And secondly, if what we were doing was just fucking to you then obviously I had you all wrong Callie. Because in my mind, we were starting something special. Maybe not the conventional way. Maybe not the right way. But I fell for you Callie. And that hasn't changed." He comes closer and he takes my hand again and pulls me to my feet.

We stand inches apart.

"I love you Callie," Matt says. The anger has gone from him now. He sounds different. Pleading almost. "Please give me a second chance and I will spend every day of my life proving to you that this is real."

My head is screaming at me to walk away from him. But how can I do that? How can I walk away from this man who stands before me, his heart on his sleeve? How can I walk away from the man I have fallen for?

"I know I fucked up, and I know why you might have your doubts about trusting me now. But ask yourself this Callie. If it was all a game, if you were nothing but the means to an end, then why am I still playing? What could I possibly have to gain by lying to you now?"

His words shatter the last remaining thread of doubt I was holding onto. Because he's right. He wouldn't have to keep up the charade now. He didn't even have to explain any of this to me. He could have just faded back out of my life as easily as he appeared in it.

I still don't have the words to explain any of this to him, and the thought of getting mixed up with a fucking billionaire scares me more than I care to admit. How long can this really last? How long before he gets sick of his Cinderella girl and trades me in for a society girl?

Matt is done waiting for words. He closes the gap between us, takes my face in his hands and looks into my eyes. "I love you," he says again.

Chapter Twenty-Five

CALLIE

His lips brush mine, and the fire bursts through me as I step closer to him, wrapping my arms around him. I promised myself this wouldn't happen; that I wouldn't let it happen, no matter what Matt said to me, and yet here it is — happening.

Matt's kiss deepens, changing from something tender and soft to something more primal. He moves his hands from my face, pushing them into my hair. I run my hands over his back and then I bring them around to the front of his body, stepping back slightly so I can work on his shirt buttons.

He begins to walk me towards the couch and I know what's coming. I know what we're going to do, and I know if I let that happen, there's no going back. It will be like me telling Matt he's forgiven, that I can give him a second chance. I don't know if I can, but my head isn't in control of me anymore. My body has taken over; I am a slave to my desire.

Matt lays me on the couch, climbing between my thighs. I wrap my legs around his waist, clutching him against me, feeling his hard cock against my pussy as he kisses down my neck.

My breathing is hard and fast as Matt's mouth moves over my neck, bringing each of my nerve endings to life. He moves back up, kissing my mouth again. I can't wait any longer. I need to feel Matt inside of me. Now. I buck my hips, moving to the side and rolling. Matt and I tumble to the floor and I land straddling his hips. I grin down on him and reach for the bottom of my dress.

As I start to peel it up my body, the apartment door opens.

"Hey bro. Oh shit, I didn't know you had company," a voice says.

I jump to my feet, pulling my dress down and then smoothing down my hair.

The fact that Matt's brother has caught us about to have sex doesn't seem to faze him in the slightest. "I'm Sebastian..."

I turn to face him, feeling my face turning red.

He grins at me. "... the handsome one."

Something about his grin is infectious and I can't help but return it. He looks similar to Matt, but they're not identical. Sebastian's hair is lighter, his eyes blue. He has the same twinkle in his eye though.

"Callie," I say. "The one you've never heard of."

"Oh, don't be so sure about that," Sebastian says. "I —"

"Seb what are you doing here?" Matt demands, cutting him off.

I glance back at Matt.

He's back on his feet, but he hasn't bothered to button his shirt back up. "We're kind of in the middle of something here."

"So I see." Sebastian smirks, looking pointedly at Matt's open shirt. He looks back at me with a wink. "I just thought I'd drop in, share a bit of brotherly love. And now I see my services are needed. I need to take this gorgeous creature and tell her all of the embarrassing things you did when you were younger."

I feel myself blush again as Sebastian describes me as a gorgeous creature. It's silly really, he's only being polite. A bit flirty sure, but nothing more.

Matt doesn't seem to think the same thing. "Just stay away from Callie, Seb. I mean it."

"She can speak for herself, you know. You don't want me to stay away from you, do you Callie?" Seb asks.

I don't even know how to answer that.

"Look now you've embarrassed her," Seb replies to Matt. Then to me, "Please excuse my brother. His social skills are pretty bad. Don't worry though, I'm available for weddings, christenings, Bar Mitzvahs. Anywhere you need someone charming really."

"Do me a favor Seb and close the door on your way out," Matt says.

"See what I mean? Appalling social skills." Seb winks at me. He heads for the door laughing. He looks back over his shoulder. "Seriously Matt, we do need to talk, but it's nothing that can't wait until the morning. Have a good night you two. And Callie? Don't do anything I wouldn't do. Not that that rules much out."

With a final chuckle, the door closes and he's gone.

"Sorry about that," Matt says. "Seb's a bit much."

"He seems fun," I say.

"That's one word for it," Matt agrees. He steps closer to me. "Now. Where were we?"

It would be easy to remind Matt exactly where we were, but Sebastian's entrance has given me a chance to get my senses back, and to think logically about this. I sit down on the couch.

Matt seems to understand that we're not going to jump right back in where we left off. He sits down beside me.

"I — I'm still a bit overwhelmed by all of this," I say. "But I understand now. I'm still pissed that you didn't tell me all of this sooner, but I get it. The thing is, I feel as though I don't know you anymore. And as much as everything in me wants to pick up where we left off, I just — I can't have sex with you tonight, Matt."

"So I guess that leaves just one question. Are you willing to get to know me all over again and give us a chance?" he asks quietly.

That is the question isn't it? But what choice do I have? It might not work with Matt and me. I might realize that this lifestyle, the money, everything that comes with it, is all too much for me. But I know I feel something for Matt. Something I've never felt for anyone. And if I walk away now without giving us a chance, I know I'll always regret it. "Yes," I say.

I see Matt's shoulders sag with relief and he smiles at me.

It's a shy smile that makes my heart soar. I think I've made the right decision. I hope I have.

Matt gets up and offers me his hand.

I take it, allowing him to pull me to my feet.

"Let's take this into the bedroom," he says.

"Matt I'm serious, I—"

He laughs and I stop talking when I realize he was joking.

"I'm just messing with you Callie. Come on. I want to show you something."

I let him lead me across his apartment and back to the window. He moves along to the end of the room and reaches out for a subtle handle I hadn't noticed. He pulls it and a panel of the glass moves to one side. I smile in delight as I step out onto a wide balcony. I move to stand with my elbows on the top of the glass barrier.

Matt stands beside me and points. "See that place there? The little restaurant?" he asks.

I look where he's pointing. Down the road from the apartment block is a small restaurant with a canopy outside and a few tables. I nod.

"When I was sixteen, I got a girlfriend. I went to my dad and asked him how I could get a raise on my allowance so I could take her on dates and stuff. You know what he told me? He said if I wanted money, I would have to get a job. I spent every Saturday and Sunday afternoon and Tuesday and Wednesday evenings washing dishes in that place."

"Really?" I ask. "It doesn't look like one of your places."

"It's not... that was another one of my dad's life lessons. He told me I had to find a job based on what I could do, not on what he could do for me."

"He sounds very wise," I say.

"Yeah. He taught me a lot about myself, about how the world works. About how anything worth having is ever easy to get, even if it looks that way from the outside. At the time, I thought he was awful. I couldn't figure out how we could have all of this money, and I had to work for a couple of dollars an hour. But now, I'm glad he stood his ground and taught me the real value of earning rather than being given."

I'm surprised once more to learn that maybe we're not all that different. I learned those same lessons as a teenager. And maybe I learned them out of necessity, where Matt learned them simply because his father didn't want him to grow up to be an entitled brat, but either way, we both knew what it was like to start at the bottom of the ladder. Maybe in some ways that was harder for Matt than me, because I knew I had no choice. He knew he had a choice, but his family wasn't ready to make his life easy.

"Four years ago, the restaurant almost went out of business. It's a little family run place. A husband and wife team, and now their two daughters. The wife got cancer, and as you can imagine, the business became less of a priority to the family. By the time she went into remission, they were so far in the red, they were on the verge of losing their home. They put that place on the market. I got wind of it and went to view it with the intention of buying it. I talked to my dad and told him I wasn't going to change a thing about it. I was going to leave the family to run it their way. I explained this to the owners. I expected them to be happy, but they refused to accept my offer. Giuseppe, the owner, told me that's not how he wanted to live his life. He wanted to support his family, but he would never be happy being answerable to anyone else. He taught me another valuable lesson. The one about working for myself instead of someone else. I'm close with my family. My brothers and I work very closely together, but I knew I needed something that was all mine, not handed down to me."

When he paused I waited as I could not take my eyes off of him.

Matt goes on to tell me the rest of it, "I bought my first restaurant after that out of money I had saved over time from my wages. It was La Trattoria. That's why this whole Marco thing felt so personal to me. It's part of the family business officially, because it's easier that way, but I have never felt so proud as I did the day I opened that front door and knew that place was mine, paid for with money I had earned. The same day, I did something else. I expected my dad to be proud of me for buying the restaurant and absolutely livid with me for the other thing. He was nonchalant about the restaurant and gave me a little lecture about how I better make it work and all that..." He trails off and looks into the distance for a moment.

Just when I think he's not going to elaborate any further he turns back and smiles at me.

"But the other thing? The thing I thought he'd drag me over the coals for? That made him proud. He told me then he knew he had raised me right."

"What did you do?" I ask.

He smiles. "I went back to Giuseppe. I told him I had learned everything I knew about working in a restaurant at his place. It was true. Until I took that job, I knew I liked cooking, but

I had no idea I would fall in love with the restaurant business. I told him I'd bought a restaurant and that it was all down to him. And then I gave him an envelope with a check inside and told him it was a thank you. It took a lot for me to convince him to accept it, but eventually, he did. He saved his business and his family was happy again."

"That's an amazing thing to do," I say. "I can see why your father was proud of you in that moment."

"I'm not telling you this to blow my own trumpet Callie. I'm telling you this because I want you to know that money doesn't have to be bad. Having money doesn't have to make someone greedy and ruthless. And I hope you can see I'm not like that. And in time, I hope you come to see that my family isn't like that either. We're pretty normal really, boring I guess you might say."

"I think you're anything but boring." I smile.

$\mathcal{I}$ look out over the city as I tell Callie more about me. She said she feels like she doesn't know me anymore, but she's willing to get to know me, so I have to open up to her. I have to tell her everything about me so she can see I am the person she's known from the start, just with a little more money and a little more power.

When I finish telling her about Giuseppe, I tell her I have some champagne in the fridge and I ask if she'd like some. She nods and I go to grab it.

I feel lighter now since I've told Callie the truth. All of it. Even the scary part. The part where I admitted that I'm in love with her. The part where she could have laughed in my face and walked away from me, taking my heart with her.

I don't just feel lucky; I feel like the luckiest man on the earth. And I meant it when I told Callie I would spend every day showing her how much I love her and who I really am. I will never, ever lie to her again, and if she'll let me, I'll hold her close to me until the day I die. I don't care how slow we have to take things. As long as she's willing to try, I'm all in.

I open the champagne and fill two glasses and then I put the bottle in an ice bucket and fill it up with ice. I'm whistling to myself as I head back to the balcony. The whistle dies in my throat when I see Callie.

She's standing where I left her, bent forward resting on the balcony wall on her elbows. Her panties are beside her on the ground, her dress around her hips and her legs spread, exposing her glistening wet pussy. My cock is hard as a rock the second I lock eyes on her. I try to speak but the words freeze in my throat and I stand in the doorway, the glasses in my hands, just drinking in the sight of this amazing woman. Finally, I find my voice. "I thought you wanted to take it slow," I say, my voice low and husky, flooded with lust.

"I changed my mind," she says. She looks back over her shoulder and grins at me. "Are you going to stand there all day, or are you going to come over here and make love to me?"

"Out here?" I ask.

"Out here," she says.

I don't need telling twice. I put the glasses down on the ground and go to her, fumbling my jeans open as I go. I slip inside of her, taking hold of her hips, moaning as I feel her wet pussy encircling my cock. I begin to thrust into her, slowly at first, wanting to make this last. The heat of her pussy makes it hard to hold myself back and I find myself moving faster within her as my desire for her takes over my brain.

I reach around to the front of her body and massage her clit, loving the way she gasps in a breath as I work her. Her hands move on the wall, gripping the top of it, her knuckles going white as I fill her with pleasure. I press down on her clit, putting more pressure, making her breath come in short gasps as her orgasm spreads through her body. I feel her pussy clench around my cock as she comes. She makes a strangled noise, holding back the scream that plays over her lips, aware that we're not exactly in the most private of places.

I grin to myself as I up my pace, slamming into her, pushing her closer to another orgasm. I wrap one hand in her hair and pull her upright. She gasps sharply, coming up with my hand, leaning back against my body, groaning with pleasure as I tug her hair again. I release it and push my hands beneath her dress, caressing her skin as I run my tongue over her neck.

I know I can't hold myself back much longer, her pussy is so fucking tight, and each thrust sends a rush of pleasure through me. I push my face against Callie's neck as a long low moan escapes me. I feel the shiver go through her body as she comes again. She throws her head back, pressing it against my shoulder, her face twisting as her orgasm seizes her. My own climax follows and I moan her name, unable to stop myself as my orgasm slams through my body, taking me and consuming me. I pull out of Callie.

She pulls her dress down and turns in my arms. She leans against me and I hold her as we get our breath back. "You are fucking amazing," I whisper into her ear. I pull my head back and find her mouth, kissing her tenderly on her lips.

She kisses me back, eager and hungry for more, her body pressed against mine, her hands beneath my shirt, caressing my back. She pulls her head back and looks into my eyes. I can see the lust in them. Her lips are slightly parted, red and swollen from the kissing. "So how about showing me your bedroom after all," she says.

I'm not about to argue with that. "Right this way ma'am." I grin as I lead Callie across the balcony, pausing long enough to grab the glasses of champagne. I hand one to Callie and raise my own. "To the balcony, the bedroom and beyond," I say.

"I'll drink to that." She laughs.

We drink and I watch Callie's throat move as she swallows. I watch her cheeks turn slightly pinker as she smiles at me. I return her smile and then I lead her through the living room area and down the hall to my bedroom door.

I push the door open and step back to let her enter first. I see her taking it all in. The nicely made bed with the black silk sheets and the black duvet cover are her main focus and I'm so relieved I changed the bed sheets just in case this happened. I don't know whether I thought it would or not really. I know the chemistry between Callie and me is strong. It always has been, but I didn't know if she'd hear me out and then walk away from me. Sometimes, I can read her like an open book, and other times, I have no idea what she's thinking.

She moves to the bed and sits on the edge of it, smiling at me. "What are you waiting for?"

"Nothing. I was just admiring the view," I say.

She blushes slightly.

I smile to myself as I close the door and cross the room to her. She sips her champagne and watches me coming towards her. Her eyes roam over my body. Her chest is rising and falling quickly, and I can see the pink flush of the skin there. I know that's not from the champagne. That's the blood rushing to the surface of her skin because she's so turned on. As turned on as I am. I wonder if she can see how hard I am for her. I bet she can. I'm making an effort to hide it from her.

She stands up as I reach her. I take her glass from her and set it down on my bedside cabinet next to my own. I pull her into my arms and she comes willingly, wrapping her arms around my waist, our lips meeting in a slow, tender kiss that fast becomes something more.

Callie's tongue is in my mouth and her hands are all over me. She tastes of champagne and I kiss her deeply, inhaling her scent, tasting her mouth, like I want to consume her. Within minutes, we've pulled each other's clothes off and I can feel Callie's skin against mine, her stomach pressing against my hard cock. God, I want this woman in every way imaginable. She drives me crazy in all the right ways.

I want to fill her up, to claim her as mine, to kiss and lick every inch of her body. I want to feel her legs around my waist, her pussy around my cock. I want to feel her sweet kisses and wrap my hands in her hair. To hold her close and never let her go. I need her to be mine.

She pulls her lips back from mine and instantly I miss the feel of her lips, the taste of her mouth.

"Sit," she commands.

I do as I'm told, giving her an amused smile. *Who am I to argue?*

Callie picks up her glass of champagne and brings it over to me. She kneels down in front of me and takes a big mouthful of the drink then she puts the glass on the floor beside her. She grabs the base of my cock and leans forward. She pushes her lips over my cock, taking me into her mouth.

I am instantly hers, like she has cast a spell over me. Her mouth is filled with champagne and the coldness takes my breath away for a second. The champagne fizzes against my skin, the bubbles causing a tickling feeling along my length as Callie bobs her head slowly, sucking me and swirling the bubbles around me with her tongue.

She swallows and the warmth of her mouth envelopes me. She moves her head faster, sucking me like she wants me as much as I want her. She moves her mouth to my tip and flicks her tongue back and forth across it. She takes another mouthful of champagne and I gasp as the temperature of her mouth plummets once more and again, I feel the delicious bubbling sensation prickling at my skin, tantalizing me, teasing me, throwing me through so many pleasurable waves at once. It's almost too much, yet at the same time, it's not enough. I need to feel her pussy wrapped around me, squeezing me, but I don't want to leave the warm wetness of her mouth.

I am close to the edge now, so close I am afraid I will go over too quickly and ruin what we're doing. I can't let myself come until I'm in her pussy, until I've taken her to Heaven and brought her back again.

I want to pull back, to get control of myself and make this last forever, but Callie is addictive and I don't want my cock to ever leave her mouth. I moan as she takes me all the way into her mouth, her hand playing with my balls, kneading them and sending shivers of delicious ecstasy through my body. I can feel the heat of her mouth again, as she swallows the champagne. I feel her throat closing and then opening again, brushing the tip of my cock and making me gasp in a tortured breath.

I thrust my hips. I want to hold back, but I can't. I can't help myself when I'm around her – she takes me to the edge so quickly, pushing me past anything I've ever felt before.

I thrust again, working my cock against her tongue and her lips. I need the release only she can give me.

She has other ideas though, and when she senses I'm about to hit the point of no return, she slips me out of her mouth, exposing my cock to the cool air.

It helps to calm me down, but at the same time, I miss those lips, her probing, licking tongue. I look down at her as I fight to get enough air, to stop my head from spinning and my cock from screaming for more.

Callie meets my eyes and smiles up at me. She runs her tongue over her lips and I moan low in my throat, knowing she's tasting me, watching her enjoy the taste. She gets to her feet and pushes my shoulders back.

I scoot backwards and she gets onto the bed, her legs straddling me. My skin comes to life where her inner thighs touch me, tingling and itching for more. She bends forward and kisses me. Her lips are slightly sticky from the champagne and she tastes as sweet as ever. I run my hands up and down her back, over her ass, cupping her cheeks and bringing her closer to me. I lightly scrape my nails down along her sides, enjoying the way she gasps slightly as I make shivers run through her body. She kisses me harder and I move my hands up her body, pushing them into her hair as she hovers above me, supporting herself on her hands and knees.

She moves back from the kiss, pulling her lips from mine and smiling down at me. Her eyes sparkle as she takes me in. She moves her mouth back out of my reach and lowers herself a little, running her hard nipples over my chest, teasing me, making trails of goose bumps burst out on my skin.

She lowers her hips, moving her slit over my cock. She moves back and forth, rubbing herself over my cock. She does it in a way that makes me want to just let go and lose control. She applies enough pressure to make my skin tingle, but not enough to bring me any sort of relief. I can tell by her panting breaths that she's teasing herself every bit as much as she's teasing me with her feather light touch.

She dips lower for a moment, pressing her mound against my cock and I suck in a rasping breath as a pulse of powerful lust floods my body.

I fight to stay in control of myself as Callie teases my body, bringing all of my senses to life. I can smell her. She smells of sweet perfume and raging pheromones, and I can smell her sweet juices, her lust.

I want to grab her shoulders, to slam her onto her back and fuck her tight little pussy, but I don't want this to be over. It's fucking agonizing, but in a delicious way.

Callie bends her head and runs her tongue across my chest. She moves her head back and then she nips my ear lobe in her teeth.

I can feel her warm breath on my ear, my neck. Does she know she's driving me absolutely crazy? I think she does. I think she knows and she's loving knowing the effect she can have on me.

She kisses down my neck and then she runs her tongue over my chest, over my nipples. She moves back to my neck and nibbles the skin there. Finally, her mouth is back on mine, but this time, she holds herself back, brushing her lips across mine so lightly, I wonder if I really felt them at all. The light touch only makes me want her more, and once more, I see myself grabbing her, throwing her down and fucking her until she's raw. I try to get the image back out of my head. It does nothing to control the fire inside of me, but now I've seen it, I can't seem to blink it away.

She straightens back up and I look at her, straddling me. That pushes the image away, but it replaces it with a better one, one that makes my cock pulse. She looks amazing, her body coated in a light sheen of sweat, her skin glowing. Her hair cascades over her shoulders and her face is flushed with desire. Her lips are parted, her breath coming faster as she rocks her hips, rubbing herself on my cock again. I can feel her juices coating me. She's so fucking wet and I need to be inside of her.

She still isn't quite ready to give us both the release we need. Instead, she reaches behind herself with one hand and encases my cock in her fist. She moves her hand up and down, slowly, teasing me more. I moan low in my throat, a moan filled with primal need. Callie smiles at me and then her fist begins to move faster and just like that, I am back on the edge. My fists grab the sheet beneath me, twisting it as pleasure floods my body. It's agony holding myself back, but I can't come yet. I have to be inside of her, to claim her pussy as mine before I let go.

I open my mouth to tell her to stop, that I need to reign myself back in, but before I can say anything, she lifts her hips and plunges herself down onto my cock. Her pussy opens for me, taking my cock into her as she comes down, impaling herself on me. I feel her tight little pussy stretching over my cock. I feel her warmth, her wet, slippery passage and it's almost too much. I bite down on the inside of my mouth, feeling the stinging pain, concentrating on that for a moment until the immense pressure in my lower stomach eases up a little.

She closes her eyes and begins to move slowly up and down on me. I can't do this. I can't take anymore teasing. My cock is screaming, every nerve ending in my whole body is screaming. I have to get some relief. I have to fuck her, hard and fast and give us both what we need.

I sit up and reach for Callie. I grab her around the waist, holding her tightly against me. I kiss the tip of her nose, her lips, and I move my hands to her shoulders and buck my hips, flipping her. She lands on her back with me on top of her. She stretches her face up to meet my kiss as she wraps her legs around my waist. She uses the soles of her feet, pressing them against my ass cheeks, pushing me further in. She moans as I fill her all the way up. I can feel her sweet, tight walls holding me fast inside of her. My moan joins hers as I move, working us both into a frenzy of passionate kisses and grabbing hands.

She is close too, I can feel her pussy tightening as I thrust into her, fast and relentless. She moans into my mouth as I move inside of her. I kiss her neck and then I look down into her lust filled eyes as her face twists and she moans again.

I keep thrusting, knowing by Callie's face that I'm hitting the right spot. She reaches behind her head with both hands, gripping the slats of the headboard in her fists. She presses her head back, exposing her flawless throat as her pussy contracts. I run my tongue up her throat and her moan becomes louder.

"Oh my God, Matt. Don't stop. Don't stop. Yes, Yes," she shouts as I pound into her.

Her words tail off becoming an unintelligible scream. I stop trying to hold myself back and I come with Callie, a powerful orgasm that slams through my whole body, pinning me in place on top of Callie as she writhes beneath me. I have never felt an orgasm as intense as this one. I can feel it in every inch of my body, pleasure exploding through me, bringing me to life in a way I've never felt before.

Her pussy is squeezing me now as she hits the peak of her climax. It holds my cock in place as I spurt into her, imprisoning me, forcing every last drop of my seed from me and into her. I spurt again, calling out Callie's name as her pussy finally relaxes. I feel my rigid muscles turn to warm jelly and I allow myself to flop down on her for a moment. She holds me against her, panting against my shoulder. I bury my face into her neck, breathing in the warm saltiness of her skin, taking a moment to feel her bare skin against mine.

Finally, I roll to the side and lay on my back beside her. I already miss her touch, the way she moans and writhes beneath me. She doesn't hold herself back when I fuck her and I like that. I like how I can send her over the edge, how I can affect her as much as she can affect me.

I can hear her trying to get herself back under control as I do the same. Our breaths come in a matching set of raspy pants. The air I suck in smells of sex, of her. It's intoxicating. I want to be able to smell her scent beside me every night for the rest of my life. I never want to let her go again. I won't let her go. I can't.

Her fingers edge closer to mine across the mattress, and I feel them against my own. I turn my hand and she slips hers into it. I hold her hand, palm to palm, and even that, the most innocence of contact makes me want her again.

When I can breathe normally again, and my muscles no longer feel like liquid, I roll onto my side and prop myself up on one elbow.

Callie turns to face me and she smiles at me.

Now, I feel like my heart will explode.

I reach out and put my palm flat on her hip and she moves closer. Her eyes are starting to close and I run my fingers gently up and down her side.

"I'm so sorry Matt," Callie mumbles, almost asleep.

"What for?" I ask her. What could she possibly be sorry for after what we've just done?

"I think I spilled champagne on your carpet," she says with a sleepy smile.

I laugh. "I can live with that. You can spill anything you want to if you do that afterwards."

She laughs softly. I move my hand, shifting slightly and putting my head on the pillow beside hers. She smiles again and I kiss her forehead. She wraps her arm around my waist and when her eyes slip closed again, they don't open. I wrap my arm around her, holding her against me, loving the heavy feeling of her arm draped across me.

I watch her sleeping, her face relaxed, her mouth open a little bit. She's so fucking beautiful. I want to kiss her back awake, make love to her again, but I don't, because I know if I wake her, I'll have to ask the question that's burning inside of me. The one I'm afraid of the answer to.

Was tonight just because she got caught up in the moment, or does it mean she's forgiven me?

Of course, I'll have to get the answer to that question at some point, but not right now.

Right now, I just want to cling to the hope inside of me and the beautiful woman beside me, and not think about anything except the way Callie feels in my arms.

Chapter Twenty-Seven

CALLIE

I wake up and stretch, wincing slightly as my back cracks. I sit up and wince again as my tender pussy presses against the mattress. I shift positions, smiling to myself as I remember last night. Matts' face was a picture when he came out onto the balcony and found me waiting for him with my dress around my hips and my panties gone.

The memory makes my clit tingle, and I turn my head, looking beside me for Matt, but he's not there. I check the time. It's only eight thirty so it's not like I've massively over-slept. Matt must have woken early and not wanted to disturb me. He could have. There are certain ways he could have woken me that I would have been more than happy about.

I promised myself I wasn't going to have sex with him until I was certain he was the same man he had always been, but apparently, I have no will power. Well no, actually that's not it. I guess I just decided that if I was going to give Matt a second chance, and we were actually going to stand a chance of making it work, then we had to do the things we had always done. And if I'm being totally honest, I just can't help myself. He turns me on so much, and the thought of being around him, but not letting him hold me or kiss me or fuck me is too much. I know I said I wanted to take things slowly, but let's be honest here. We're already way past that point.

I'm still not really sure about this whole thing. I mean don't get me wrong, I think I can get past what's happened, especially now I know my promotion was nothing to do with Matt. That bothered me more than him hiding his identity from me. It felt too close to whoring myself out.

Last night, Matt was sweet and attentive, which in fairness... he always has been. And I know he's making a real effort to open up to me. He told me several personal stories last night. I guess my issue isn't with him, it's with me. I worry that we're just too different. Not as people, as people, we're pretty similar. But our life experiences are worlds apart, and I don't know if we can get past that.

I don't see myself ever fitting into Matt's world. And right now, he might like the idea of being with a bit of rough, but for how long? But what about his family? It's one thing for him to say they're down to earth and all that, but how are they going to react when they find out he's seeing Jane Nobody? Will they think I'm just some opportunistic little gold digger, or will they humor me, let Matt have his Cinderella moment and then move on with his life?

I sigh and stand up. I told him I was willing to give us a chance, and I meant it. I have to put these thoughts to one side, take it one day at a time, and just see how it goes. It's hard though. It's hard to take things slow when you love someone. And I'm afraid to let myself love him in case I lose him.

My stomach growls and I shake my head. Why am I always so damned hungry? I look around for my clothes. I see Matt's shirt and slip that on instead. It covers me to my mid-thigh and it'll work nicely for breakfast. I fasten up enough buttons to cover myself and I move through to the living room, humming to myself.

Ok I admit it. I'm happy. Being with Matt makes me happy, so I'm going to let go of everything else and just focus on that. Surely, when all is said and done, that's all that really matters.

I spot a plate piled high with food and a glass of orange juice on the kitchen counter and I move closer. The plate has two croissants, some strawberries, and a huge pile of bacon. Beside it is a note which I pick up and read.

Callie,

Sorry, something came up and I had to go to work. There's fresh coffee in the pot. I've left you breakfast out, but help yourself to anything else you want.

Matt x

Anything else? Holy shit, how much does he think I can eat? I can't help but laugh as I go to the coffee pot and pour myself a cup. I take it back to the seat I sat in last night at the dining table so I can sit and look out over the city. I grab a croissant and a few of the strawberries. I tell myself that's enough, and then I reconsider and take two rows of bacon too. I've eaten the bacon and the strawberries, and I'm halfway through the croissant when I hear the door open.

"How was work?" I ask.

"Perfect babe," a voice that isn't Matt's answers me. "How sweet of you to ask."

I turn around quickly, wondering who the hell it is. I feel a stab of fear which disappears when I see Sebastian.

He walks towards the kitchen and pours himself a mug of coffee. "Nice shirt," he comments.

"Thanks. I like yours as well." I grin.

"Yeah? I think mine would look better on you," he says.

I feel heat rising to my cheeks. Partly because of Sebastian's comment and partly because I am suddenly extremely conscious of the fact I'm not wearing any underwear.

I'm pleased when Sebastian sits down opposite me with his coffee. At least now the table hides my lower half and the shirt is buttoned high enough to cover my breasts. "So what brings you here so early?" I ask.

"Well, I wanted to see you obviously." Sebastian winks. "I wanted to make sure you hadn't been a figment of my imagination."

I roll my eyes and he laughs.

"Okay, seriously, I was hoping to catch Matt before he left for work. Is he still in bed?"

"No, he's already left," I say.

"And yet, you're still here. So it must be serious. Does that mean I've missed my chance to steal you away?" Sebastian says.

I don't even know how to begin to answer that. Of course, I'm not going to let him steal me away as he so eloquently puts it, but are Matt and I serious? I just don't know, and I'm certainly not going to start debating it with Sebastian.

"Hey, I'm just joking," Sebastian says when I don't answer. "I'm not really in the habit of trying to steal my brother's girlfriend. Unless of course she wants me to, and then that's different isn't it? It's almost like a public service."

I feel the corners of my lips turn up slightly. His girlfriend. That's the only part I focus on. Matt said that to his brother? That I'm his girlfriend. Or has Sebastian just decided that for himself because I'm still here?

Sebastian grins at my confusion and shakes his head. "Well, it looks like that was news to you. Typical Matt. If he can't tell you, then I will, because I have a good feeling about you. I think you might just be a keeper. Matt is serious about you Callie. You know how much he loves the restaurant right?"

I nod, still trying to process the part where Sebastian is so certain Matt is serious about me.

"He insisted on running the whole operation himself to get the manager caught red handed. But he was willing to throw it all away once he met you. He was so scared you'd hate him once you found out the truth. You don't do you?"

"Hate him? No, of course not," I say.

"Well, I figured that seeing as you're wearing his shirt, but women are weird so I just thought I'd check." He grins. "You know, just in case you're not that into him but you have some sort of shirt fetish."

"I'm only a little bit weird." I laugh. "And I'm more of a belt fetishist."

I can feel myself warming to Sebastian. I wasn't sure of him at first. He seemed cocky and so self-assured the way he swanned in and started flirting with me like he'd known me all of his life. But underneath it all, he seems to really care about Matt. And I love the fact that Matt has talked to his brother about me. It gives me the reassurance I needed that he did care about me the whole time. "So..." I say with a wicked grin. "Do you have any embarrassing stories about Matt as a kid?"

"Oh hundreds," Sebastian says with a twinkle in his eye.

By the time I've finished my breakfast, I've heard about the time Matt got himself locked in the bathroom, and by the time his dad managed to get him out, he had emptied three full bottles of bubble bath into the tub. Sebastian laughed, telling me how long it took his mom to get rid of all of the bubbles. I've heard about what he was like in school, a bit of geek according to Sebastian, but I find that hard to believe, and about the time Matt came home with a stray dog, announced he had adopted it, and threw a fit two hours later when the frantic owners tracked it down and came to collect it.

"Right then, I'll leave you to your day." Sebastian smiles as he gets up, takes his cup through to the kitchen and puts it in the sink.

"I'll tell Matt you dropped by," I say.

"No need. It wasn't anything that can't wait."

I stand up to see Sebastian out, remembering too late that I'm only wearing Matt's shirt. It's too late to sit back down without drawing even more attention to the fact I'm pretty much naked, so I brazen it out and walk to the door, acting casual like this isn't phasing me in the least.

"See you later, Callie," Sebastian says as he opens the door. "Oh and by the way. What I said earlier about not being in the habit of stealing my brother's girlfriend? That could change if you keep wearing shit like that around me." He winks at me and laughs.

I just stand there open mouthed.

"Later," he calls over his shoulder from the hallway.

"Bye." I laugh as I close the door and stand with my back against it for a moment. Sebastian is a handful, but something tells me underneath it all he's harmless. I decide to go shower and get back into my own clothes. Just in case he comes back, or some other family member drops in unannounced. I find my panties on the balcony, blushing slightly as I retrieve them, and then I get the rest of my things from the bedroom. I shower and dress then I sit on Matt's bed towel drying my hair.

I debate calling Chloe, but what would I tell her? I'm still not entirely sure where Matt and I stand. I should probably go, but it's only now that it occurs to me that I have absolutely no idea where Matt keeps his spare front door key. I can hardly leave and leave the place unlocked, although Matt seems to have no such qualms as that's twice in two days Sebastian has strolled in and caught me in various states of undress.

Chapter Twenty-Eight

CALLIE

$\mathcal{I}$ wash my breakfast plates and put the leftovers in the fridge and then I take my glass of orange juice and go back out onto the balcony. It's good I don't have any classes today I think to myself as I sit looking out over the city, listening to the faraway sound of the traffic on the streets below.

By the time I've finished my orange juice, I have managed to work myself up into an agitated state. What if Matt didn't really have to go to work? What if he realized this was a mistake and he'd left early, hoping I'd take the hint and just leave? What if he comes back and he's angry that I'm still here?

I try to remember him telling me he loves me, Sebastian telling me he's serious about me, but all I can focus on now is whether or not it's weird that I'm still here. God, no wonder Matt didn't bring me here sooner. He was probably scared of this very thing. Like he brings me here once and I just don't leave.

I stand up abruptly and go and get my handbag. I pull my phone out and text Matt. *Hey. Where's your key? I don't want to leave your door unlocked.*

That gives him the perfect opportunity to tell me where the key is and let me know he wants me to leave. It also explains why I'm still here so late without making it weird. A reply pings in and I feel my stomach knot slightly when it hits me that I don't want to leave. I open the message.

Do you need to leave right now? I'm almost done and I was kind of hoping you'd be there when I got back. If you do need to go, the key is in the top drawer next to the sink in the kitchen x.

I can't keep the smile from my face. He wants me to be here when he gets back. And he signed off with a kiss, which is more than I did. I text him back.

I'll be here x.

I wander back inside and rinse my glass and then I go and sit down and turn the TV on. Daytime TV is the worst, but it's not like I'll be able to concentrate on anything anyway. Not now since I know Matt wants me here. Not since I know it's all real.

It's almost time for lunch when the door opens again. I look up and smile when Matt comes in.

He beams when he sees me. "I'm so glad you stayed," he says as he crosses the room and kisses me hello.

"Me too," I say.

He sits down beside me and pulls my feet into his lap. "I planned on taking today off to spend with you, but I got a call this morning, something I couldn't ignore." He's smiling and he looks quite pleased with himself.

"Go on," I urge.

"Stewart, the new manager in the restaurant called HR and asked for my number. They refused to give it to him and tried to find out what was wrong, but he refused to talk to anyone but me. They called me with his number and he asked me to go down there straight away. He wouldn't talk over the phone, but I could hear in his voice something was wrong. I went down there expecting the worst."

"And?" I prompt him when he pauses.

"And he showed me some papers he found tucked away in the back of the safe. He said they showed some unusual activity, and he wanted to talk to me personally because he was afraid he would be blamed for it all. I assured him that wouldn't be the case. The papers were pretty much the proof I needed that Marco was laundering money through the restaurant."

I grin. "That's great news. So what happens now?"

"I've spoken to my lawyer and delivered the papers to him, so now we wait and let him work his magic I guess. He's confident this will end in a conviction."

"That's great," I say.

"There's something else as well, but you have to promise not to get mad okay?"

The second he says it I feel myself preparing to be mad. If someone makes you promise not to be mad, it means they've done something they know for a fact is going to piss you off. "What have you done Matt?" I demand.

"You haven't promised," he says.

"And I'm not going to until you tell me what you've done."

"I spoke to Sasha," he says.

Ok, I was imagining something much worse than that and I relax a little. "Why would I be mad about that?" I ask.

"Well we were talking about what went down, and then of course we got on to you, and I might have laid into her a little bit. It just pissed me off that your so called friends were so quick to think the worst of you and I made it known."

"Oh," I say.

"That's it? Oh?" Matt looks surprised.

I shrug. "What else is there to say?"

"I told her you knew nothing about any of it, and she seemed like she was genuinely sorry. She asked me to ask you to call her," he adds.

"Screw that," I say. Now I am kind of mad. "She didn't believe me when I told her, but now you say it, she believes it and expects me to go running after her? I don't think so."

"Now you're mad," Matt says, watching my face carefully.

"I am." I pull my feet away from him and get to my knees on the couch, so I can lean in and kiss him. "But not with you."

"I kind of thought it might be a whole *I don't need anyone to fight my battles for me* kind of a reaction," he says.

"I don't need anyone to fight my battles," I confirm, smiling at him. "But I think it's sweet that you want to. You know what? Life's too short to be bitter. I will call Sasha. We'll never be friends like we used to be. I could never trust her again, but I'm not going to hold onto a stupid grudge." I get up and go and get my phone. I go out onto the balcony and call Sasha.

She picks up almost immediately. "Callie. I'm so glad you called. I'm so sorry," she gushes.

"It's fine," I say, my tone neutral. And it really is fine, because everything has worked out for the best. I got out of a job I didn't particularly love, and I have Matt.

"I know you think I only believe you now because of what Matt said, but it's not like that," Sasha says.

"No?" I ask, raising an eyebrow.

"No," she confirms. "I realized you were telling the truth pretty much the moment after I was such a bitch to you. But then you walked out before I could apologize, and I know I should have called you, but I was so afraid you wouldn't take my call, and then too long had passed you know?"

"Honestly, it's fine. I get it," I say. I feel myself thawing a little as I picture Sasha nibbling on her nail like she does when she's nervous. "I was plenty pissed at the time, but the more I thought about it, the more I realized I would have found it hard to believe that someone didn't know their boyfriend's true identity myself."

"So you and Matt are still together then huh? Tell me all of the details," she says.

Now I picture her eyes sparkling as she demands the details of my love life. I find myself sitting down and telling her how I wasn't sure I could move on from what happened, but that I did. I tell her the most important thing; how happy being with Matt makes me. And really, that's all that matters.

We end the call promising to stay in touch with each other. I think we both know deep down we probably won't. There'll be the odd text message back and forth at first, and then they'll slowly fade out. But still, I'm glad we made up.

I go back inside where Matt is waiting for me.

"Do you want to go out and get some lunch?" he says.

"I thought you'd never ask. I'm starving." I smile.

He gets up.

"I need to go to my dorm and get changed first though," I say.

He shakes his head and comes over to me. He pulls me into his arms and kisses me. "Callie, you look amazing as you are." He smiles.

"You know, maybe we should skip lunch and go and get your eyes tested instead." I laugh.

"If we're skipping lunch, I have a better idea of what we can do instead," he says.

I feel a warm rush in my pussy, and I know it won't be lunch we're eating today. "Really? What's that?" I ask, playing along.

"Well, I was thinking I could take you back into the bedroom and show you something," he says.

"Show me something, huh?" I grin, looking down at his cock.

He laughs. "That's not what I meant, but I'd be happy to show you that too."

"What did you mean then?"

"I want to show you that I love you. Now and forever," he says, serious again.

"I love you too, Matt," I say.

And I know it's true. I really do. And everything else? The worries, the baggage, the money? We'll just have to deal with it all as it comes.

Together.

Chapter Twenty-Nine

MATT

"*S*orry I'm late," Callie says as she gets into the car. She wraps her arms around my neck and kisses me loudly on the cheek.

"It's fine," I say with a grin. "I know what you're like once you get in that place."

She laughs. "What can I say? I love books and I love working at the library. I honestly don't know why I didn't think of applying there sooner."

I pull away from the curb and head towards my apartment. Callie chats away, telling me about her day. I'm listening, but I'm not really hearing her. I'm too nervous to pay as much attention as I should be.

"Are you listening to me?" she demands, her eyes narrow as she studies me.

It's as though she can read my mind at times I swear. "Yup. Someone brought a book back that was three months overdue and then they couldn't understand why you weren't able to waive the late fee."

"Oh, you were listening." She smiles. "You just seemed like you were a million miles away."

"Things aren't always what they seem." I grin. I tell myself I need to hide my nervous energy better in the future. I almost ruined the surprise.

We reach my apartment and go in. "So you know in the car when you thought I was a million miles away?" I say.

Callie eyes me suspiciously and nods.

"Well, I kind of was. Because I was thinking about your face when you see your gifts," I say with a grin. "They're on the bed."

She frowns, but it's a good natured frown. "Matt, we talked about this and you agreed not to spend too much money on me," she chastises me.

"Ahh, but we never did specify an amount. How much is too much? Nothing is too much in my mind." I grin.

She punches me in the arm.

I laugh. "It's our five-month anniversary. That means I'm allowed to treat you."

Callie's face softens. "You remembered."

"Of course I did." I take her hand. "Now come on and open your presents."

She lets me lead her to the bedroom and she moves to the bed. She picks up the smallest gift first and opens it. Her face lights up when she sees the diamond earrings. "Oh Matt, they're beautiful," she whispers. "But you really —"

"— shouldn't have," I finish for her. "But I did. Now are you going to ruin the moment by lecturing me, or are you just going to enjoy your new things?"

She reaches for my hand and pulls me onto the bed beside her. She kisses me full on the mouth. "Thank you," she says when she pulls her mouth from mine.

I know it's killing her to not remind me about our agreement, but it kills me every day to not be able to treat her how she deserves to be treated, and this is my compromise. I'll respect her wishes on a day to day basis, but on special occasions, I get to spoil her.

She opens the gift with the bracelet and necklace to match her earrings. Finally, she moves onto the biggest box. She lifts the lid and pushes aside the tissue paper and lifts out the red silk dress. She stands up and holds it against herself, twirling around and giggling like a schoolgirl. "I love it. I love it all. Thank you!"

"I thought maybe you could wear it tonight," I say.

"Oh, really? And where might we be going?" she asks.

"My mom invited us over for dinner. My dad's away on business, but my mom is dying to meet you. Seb and Chance will be there too."

She sits down and peers at me. "You want me to meet your family?"

I laugh at how surprised she looks. "Of course I do. The only reason it's taken this long is because I know you're nervous about meeting them."

She nods. "Okay."

I kiss her. "Don't worry Callie. Honestly, if you can handle Seb, you can handle anything. Chance is much more reserved and the only thing you'll have to worry about with my mom is that she'll want to make you a part of the family the instant she meets you."

Chapter Thirty

CALLIE

To say I'm nervous as I get out of the Uber at Matt's parents' place would be the understatement of the century. His parents' house is huge and I'm already overwhelmed just looking at it.

Matt takes my hand in his. "Look we'll show our faces and if you don't want to stick around, I'll make something up and we'll leave early."

I try to relax as I shake my head, telling myself I have to make the effort for him. "It's okay. I'll be okay. Do I look all right?"

"You look perfect." Matt smiles.

I feel good in the dress, accessorized with the diamonds he bought me, but feeling like I've made the effort still does nothing to settle my nerves as Matt leads me up the steps to the front door.

He opens the door and we step in.

"Mom? We're here," he calls.

She appears instantly, an apron covering a beautiful midnight blue dress. Her hair is swept up in a French pleat and she looks younger than I pictured her. Most importantly, she doesn't look me up and down like I imagined she would. Instead, she comes towards us, beaming, her arms outstretched. She hugs Matt and then me. I feel myself relaxing slightly.

"This is Callie, Mom," Matt says.

"It's a pleasure to meet you Mrs. Hunter." I say.

"The pleasure is mine dear, and it's Eve. Carlton sends his apologies, but he couldn't get out of the trip. I hope you understand. Come on in, don't be shy," she says, ushering me towards the living room. "You already know Sebastian, but you need to meet Chance."

I allow myself to be swept away by her chatter and I find myself in a tasteful living room. Sebastian and a younger man I assume is Chance both get to their feet as we enter.

"Looking good as usual Callie." Sebastian winks at me.

"Can you give it a rest for just one night?" Matt groans.

"What? You don't think she looks good?" Sebastian says.

Matt just scowls at him.

"I'm Chance, the normal one." Chance grins at me, stepping forward and extending his hand.

"Callie," I reply, shaking his hand.

He has Matt's smile, but his complexion is fair, his hair blonde and cut in a trendy tousled style.

"Dinner won't be long. Sebastian, why don't you come on through and grab Matthew and Callie some drinks?" Eve says.

I have a feeling she does it to keep him away from me, so he can't keep pissing Matt off.

The dinner goes well, and by the end of it, I am completely stuffed full, but more importantly, I feel relaxed. Eve is the perfect hostess, drawing me out of myself and making me feel welcome. Matt was right. Within ten minutes in her company, I am made to feel like one of the family. Sebastian spent dinner flirting with me and getting dirty looks off Matt. Chance was much quieter; he seems shy but friendly.

"I'm so sorry to eat and run, but I really do have to go," Chance says, getting up.

"Got a hot date waiting?" Matt teases him.

"No such luck. Just work stuff," Chance says.

"Yeah Matt, we can't all have hot dates to bring to dinner," Sebastian says, grinning at me.

I laugh and shake my head as Matt rolls his eyes.

Chance says his goodbyes and Eve sees him out. She comes back in. "Matthew darling, if you're finished, would you mind getting started on the dishes?"

Matt was right about that as well. His family is normal. Down to earth. I kind of expected a waiter, a chef and a maid to clean up afterwards, but Eve had cooked herself and now, like my own mom would, she expects her children to help her clean up.

Matt nods and gets to his feet.

I stand up too. "I'll give you a hand."

"No Callie, sit down. You're a guest," Eve says.

"As am I." Matt grins.

"I could think of other words to describe you." Eve laughs.

"Honestly, let me help. It'll do me good to move around and work off some of that pudding." I laugh.

Matt and I go through to the kitchen and Matt begins to fill the sink. I can hear Eve asking Sebastian to make Martinis.

"Did you notice?" Matt asks.

"Notice what?" I ask as Matt begins to wash the dishes.

"I took the last roast potato when no one was looking!" He laughs.

"That's shocking!" I giggle as I pick up the plate Matt has washed and dry it, setting it down on the table behind me when I realize I have no idea where it goes.

Sebastian comes in soon after with our drinks. "Wouldn't you rather be sitting in the living room with me, Callie?" He grins.

"Nope." I laugh.

He puts his hand to his heart. "Ouch. I'm hurt!" He chuckles as he leaves the room.

"I'm sorry about him. I'll have words with him," Matt says, his tone sharp.

I look up seeing the frown on his face. "It's fine Matt, don't say anything to him. It's just a bit of fun, and I honestly don't mind it."

"He never used to be like this you know. I mean he was never shy, but he wasn't quite so over the top. He had his heart broken a few years ago and it changed him. He flirts like that with everyone, outrageously almost. I think it's a defense mechanism, so no one wants to get too close to him anymore.

He's a serial flirt, a serial dater. But he doesn't let himself get serious with anyone. He claims he just isn't ready to settle down, but it's more than that. He's afraid of getting hurt again."

"One day, he'll meet the right girl and he'll see that she was worth waiting for," I say.

"I hope so." Matt picks up his drink and hands me mine.

We clink glasses and take a drink. It's strong but it's good.

"He sure makes a mean Martini, I'll give him that much," Matt says.

We finish the dishes and go to the living room where we join Sebastian and Eve. We chat for a bit.

After an hour, Sebastian stands up. "I'm going to message for an Uber. Do you guys want to share?"

Matt looks at me and I shrug. I don't mind either way.

"Yeah, that would be great." Matt nods.

Sebastian goes off to arrange the Uber.

Eve smiles at me. "It's been lovely to meet you Callie. Hopefully, we'll see you more often, since now you know we don't bite."

I feel myself blushing and I nod. It seems so stupid now that I was so afraid to meet Matt's family.

"You two will have to come over for dinner one day next week when your dad's home Matthew," Eve adds.

"We will," Matt says. "Or better yet, why don't you come over to my apartment and I'll cook?"

"You're only saying that because you know the next time Callie comes over, the embarrassing baby photos are coming out." Eve laughs.

"Well yeah, exactly." Matt shakes his head at her.

"The Uber's here," Sebastian calls from the hallway.

We all say our goodbyes with hugs, *nice to have met you* and promises to do it all again soon.

"So you survived your first trip to the lion's den," Sebastian says, turning in his seat to look at Matt and me in the back. "Next time, you know she'll be talking about marriage and babies. You're her last hope Callie. I mean I'm a lost cause and Chance is a workaholic."

"And yet strangely, she's subtler than you are," Matt says.

Sebastian shrugs. "Not for long. Mark my words." He directs the Uber driver to pull up at the next corner. "See you later Matt. Callie, always a pleasure. Call me anytime you get bored with him and want a date with the fun brother."

"Noted." I laugh.

He closes the door.

Matt tells the Uber driver where to go and then he goes quiet.

I nudge him gently with my shoulder. "Don't let him get to you, Matt. It's all in fun."

"What?" Matt says. "Oh, it's not him. I was just thinking."

"Oh, do tell." I grin.

"I was just wondering how I got so lucky as to have you here with me now, putting up with my brother's shit and laughing about it."

I think there's more to it than that. He looks worried, but I let it go and rest my head on his shoulder. He takes my hand in both of his and traces little patterns on the palm with his fingertips.

We reach Matt's apartment and head up in the elevator. Matt seems to be getting more agitated by the second.

I can't ignore it any longer. "Come on, spill it," I say.

He shakes his head. "When we get inside."

Oh God, this is it isn't it? It was all an act. His mom has told him to get rid of the pauper. We get out of the elevator and I step into Matt's apartment with a lead weight in my stomach. The second he closes the door I whirl to face him. "Okay, out with it," I say.

He nods and takes my hand, leading me out onto the balcony.

I start to calm down a little bit. Who takes someone onto the balcony to dump them? Maybe Sebastian told him something work related that he's worrying about. Matt turns to face me and he smiles and the worry floats away.

"I was just looking at you and thinking of how beautiful you are, but then I realized something was missing," he says.

"Missing?"

He nods solemnly. "Yes. I have one more gift for you. One I really hope you'll accept."

He reaches into his pocket and brings his hand out.

His fist closed so I can't see what he's holding.

"I love you, Callie. More than I ever thought it was possible to love another human being." He drops to one knee and I gasp as he opens his fist and reveals the little box there.

He opens the box and shows me a diamond ring that matches my other new jewelry. "Would you make me the happiest man in the world and agree to be my wife?"

I can hardly see for the tears that blur my vision. "Yes. Yes, of course I'll marry you!"

He pushes the ring onto my finger. It's a perfect fit, just like Matt and me. He gets to his feet.

I lift my hand, smiling as I see the ring there. "I love you so much, Matt."

He pulls me into his arms and as our lips meet, I know for sure that this is forever. I have found my prince, my knight, my soul mate. And I have never been happier than I am in this moment.

EPILOGUE

Callie

I clap my hands in delight and spin around the second the door closes as the porter leaves.

"Oh Matt, it's perfect," I say, looking around the room I'm standing in.

"You sound surprised," Matt laughs.

I laugh with him and shake my head.

"No. I'm not surprised that it's nice. I'm just excited to even be here," I say.

I still can't quite believe this is happening to me. When Matt told me he had booked us a surprise romantic get away, I expected a couple of days in Paris or something similar. Instead, we're spending two weeks in Dubai.

I move across the room to Matt and he pulls me into his arms. I look up into his face and he looks back down at me, his eyes shining with love as he looks at me. I am so happy, I feel as though I might burst and I still have to keep pinching myself to make sure this is all real. There's still a little part of me that is convinced that I'm going to wake up and find out that Matt and me, our moving in together, all of it, has just been a dream and I'm still single and alone.

I squeeze Matt a little bit tighter, needing to make sure he's real and that he's not just going to float away from me at any moment. He smiles at me and leans down and rubs his lips over mine.

"So what do you want to do first?"he asks.

I move out of his embrace and go to sit on the edge of the large bed.

"I thought maybe we could start with an early night," I say. Matt grins at me and I bite my lip to hide my own grin and then I go on. "I'm pretty tired after all of that travelling."

The grin falters slightly on Matt's face as I add on the last part.

"Oh. Right. Ok. Yeah," Matt says, seemingly unable to put a full sentence together through his disappointment and even though I bite my lip again, I can't stop myself from laughing this time.

"I'm joking," I say, patting the spot beside me on the bed. "Get over here."

Matt doesn't need telling twice. He closes the gap between us as I scoop backwards on the bed. Matt gets on the bed with me and our lips touch again. This time, it's a long, passionate kiss that makes my insides swirl and my pussy tighten. Within moments, our clothes have all been shed and I can feel Matt's hot skin against mine. The feeling of his naked body touching mine sends me wild with desire and I want him so badly.

I reach down and wrap my hand around his hard cock, rubbing it up and down. Matt moans, his breath warm against my ear. He kisses down my neck, sending shivers of desire through me as his fingers probe between my lips and find my clit. We work each other simultaneously, our breaths becoming ragged together. I can feel my climax creeping up on me, and I want to come so badly, to get the release my body needs to bring me fully to life.

I press myself against Matt's fingers, pressing onto them hard and moving back and forth across them. Heat spreads through my body as my clit tingles deliciously. I stop moving my fist although I don't release my hold on Matt's cock. I am consumed by the pleasure that's starting to assault me, barely even aware that I am still now.

Pleasure courses through my body, a wave of ecstasy that catches me off guard in its intensity, pushing me over the edge with a force that leaves me breathless. I can feel my whole body coming to life, fireworks of tingles exploding throughout me. I try to breathe, try to swallow, but I can't do either. I am suspended in nothingness for a moment, just a nerve ending, frozen in time and space as Matt's magic fingers keep pressing down on my clit.

After an agonizing but delicious couple of minutes, Matt releases my sensitive clit and the orgasm begins to fade, allowing me to breathe once more. I gasp in a breath that expands my lungs and sends more fire through my body and then I am panting as my orgasm slowly leaves me.

My clit is tingling, my pussy clenching, desperate to be filled by Matt. Matt smiles down at me as I recover from my climax and then he leans in and rubs his lips gently over mine in a light and gentle kiss, teasing me. I push my hand into his hair, bringing his face hard against mine, kissing him ferociously. My other hand is still wrapped around his cock, and I guide him to my opening. He moans into my mouth as the tip of his cock runs through my slit, spreading my juices around.

His hand covers mine, pushing his cock to the edge of my pussy and we both remove our hands as Matt slams into me, filling me up and making me moan with pleasure as he starts to move inside of me.

I wrap my legs around his waist and my arms round his shoulders, clutching him to me as we become one together. He moves inside of me, faster and faster, and I know he's not far from reaching his own climax. I clench my pussy, tightening myself around him and he moans my name in a low, husky voice that sends a rush of liquid from me.

As Matt's cock brushes over my g-spot, I can feel another orgasm building inside of me, the heat inside of my belly just waiting to explode through my body. Matt is moving faster and faster now, and I can't hold myself back any longer. My orgasm floods me once more, waking up tired muscles and spreading fire through me.

I cling to Matt, my nails digging into his shoulders as I am carried away on a wave of intense pleasure. I am still aware of Matt moving inside of me, but nothing else registers. It's like it's just Matt and me, floating on a cloud of air, nothing in the universe real except the two of us and this insane pleasure.

I make a whimpering sound as my pleasure pulses down my limbs and my pussy goes wild, clenching and spasming around Matt.

My orgasm is just starting to release me from its fiery grip when Matt pumps into me one last time, filling me right up and then spurting his hot desire into me. I cling to him as he presses his face against my neck and whispers my name. I feel his cock pulsing inside of me and then I feel another rush of heat and then he's pulling out of me.

He rolls off me and we lay side by side, panting, our fingers entwined in each other's. And in that moment, it still feels like we're the only two people in the world, and I know that if that was the case, I would still be the happiest woman to have ever lived. How could I not be when I am with my soul mate?

"So, how much of the city do you reckon we'll be seeing?" Matt asks me after we have recovered slightly.

I laugh softly as I roll closer to him and drape my arm across his waist.

"Not much if I get my way," I say, my hand already moving lower over his stomach.

"Your wish is my command," Matt says as we come back together, our lust still every bit as explosive now as it was the first time we ever made love. "I love you Callie."

"I love you too," I whisper. "Always and forever."

he End

COMING SOON...

Want to read more about the Hunter Brothers?
Sebastian's story is next...

Chapter Thirty-One

CHAPTER 1

Sebastian

I take a subtle look at the woman standing next to me at my front door. She's saying something, something I don't hear, and then she giggles, not seeming to notice or care that I don't respond.

She's drunk, but not so drunk that I'm taking advantage of her by bringing her back to my place. It was her who kept ordering more cocktails after the work dinner. It was her who slipped her shoes off beneath the table and ran her toes up my leg inside of my trousers. She might be a little bit tipsy, but she knows exactly what she wants. Me.

She's tall. Almost as tall as me, and she holds herself with confidence. A lot of tall women slouch, wanting to not stand out, but not Natalie. No, Natalie wants to be seen, to be noticed. Well she's going to love tonight because fuck me I see her. I see her willowy waist, her full breasts and her long legs. I see the lust in her eyes and the glisten of moisture on her lips where she keeps licking them seductively.

Oh I see her alright, and pretty soon, I'll be seeing a whole lot more of her. Natalie catches me watching her as I miss the lock with the key. She smiles, a smile that sends a blast of fire through me. It's the smile of a predator about to devour their prey. I'm good with that. I am most definitely open to being devoured by that sensual mouth of hers.

"Is something distracting you Sebastian?" she asks, faking innocence even as she tugs at her top, revealing a little more cleavage.

I let out a soft laugh.

"Whatever gave you that impression?"

"I thought maybe you were thinking about our potential merger," Natalie smiles putting all of the emphasis on the merger.

I finally manage to unlock the door. It's not the smooth move I would have liked, but it sure doesn't seem to have put Natalie off. I can almost smell the lust coming off her in waves.

"Oh I think our merger is a sure thing," I reply as I step inside my house and stand aside so Natalie can enter.

She laughs and twiddles a strand of her silvery blonde hair around one finger. She looks down for a second and then looks up at me through her lashes, her smile widening.

"How about the tour first?" she asks.

"Sure," I grin.

I would have preferred to have gotten straight down to business so to speak. It's not like Natalie was going to be anything other than a one night stand. Why does she want to see every room of my house? The only room she needs to see is my bedroom. Still, it won't take too long. Why not?

"So what's down there?" she asks, pointing to a door off the hallway with a set of wooden steps leading down to a basement.

"Oh that's where I keep the bodies of those who have double crossed me," I laugh.

"No seriously? What's down there?" she pouts. "I bet it's a flashy wine cellar isn't it?"

"Not exactly," I laugh. "I'm more of a bourbon man."

When it's clear to me she isn't going to relent and just let me whisk her off to the bedroom, I bite back the sigh and lead her to the stairs. I lead her down, pulling on the light as I step inside the door. Natalie laughs when we reach the bottom of the stairs and she sees the room.

The basement covers the entire length and width of my house in one room, and I've made it into a games room. There's a full size pool table, several pinball machines, a dart board and a few video game machines. There's also a well stocked bar in the corner, several high stools lining it, and half a dozen bean bags scattered around the room. I decide to make the most of the tour. I head for the bar and pour out two large bourbons. I hand one to Natalie who sips it and makes a face and then laughs.

"It's strong," she says.

"What can I say? I thought I'd get you drunk and take advantage of you," I grin.

"Works for me," she laughs.

I begin to relax a little as I sip the bourbon. Natalie is a sure thing. She hasn't asked for the tour because she's having second thoughts. She's just nosey. I can deal with nosey.

"So, do you want to continue the tour or do you want me to kick your ass at pool first?" I ask.

She glances over at the pool table and then she smiles and shakes her head.

"The rest of the tour sounds good. I can do without the humiliation of being thrashed at pool," she says.

I lead the way back upstairs.

"Yeah people say I'm pretty good with my balls," I say, looking back over my shoulder and winking at Natalie.

"Oh I bet you are," she grins back.

I reach the top of the stairs and take her into the lounge. It's a reasonable sized room, with brown leather sofas, an entertainment system, a coffee table, and little else.

"Wow you like the whole minimalist thing don't you?" Natalie remarks.

"What more would I need in here?" I ask, genuinely curious as to what she thinks is missing.

"I don't know. The little things that make a house a home," she says. She smiles. "This is such a bachelor pad. You need a woman's touch."

"The only place I need a woman's touch is ..." I trail off, nodding towards my crotch.

Natalie laughs and shakes her head, but she moves closer to me. I can smell the bourbon fumes on her breath when she whispers into my ear.

"That can definitely be arranged."

"You know what?" I say. "Let's finish the tour right here. The kitchen is a kitchen. Normal. Boring. My office is a no go area. So we may as well just head upstairs right now."

I don't wait for her to respond. I turn and walk from the lounge, heading for the stairs. I know she's following me, eager to get to the good bit herself now. I reach the top of the stairs and lead her along another hallway.

"Bathroom. Linen closet," I say pointing out doors as we pass them. "Spare bedroom. Another spare bedroom."

"You know if you get bored of the corporate world, you would make an excellent tour guide," she laughs.

"I aim to please," I reply.

I reach the end of the hallway and stop outside of the final door. I throw it open with a flourish.

"And the only room you really wanted to see. My bedroom."

Natalie gives me another one of those lust filled grins that makes my cock twitch, and steps into the bedroom. She looks around for a moment and then nods her approval. Obviously the addition of a wardrobe and a chest of drawers makes this room more suitably furnished to Natalie's tastes. She misses the point in my opinion. It's all still practical stuff. There is nothing in this room that distinguishes it from a soulless hotel room.

"Are you going to stand in the doorway all night then or are you coming in?" Natalie asks.

She downs the last of her bourbon and puts the glass down on the chest of drawers. I step into the room and kick the door closed behind me. The moonlight streaming in the window gives us enough light to see by and I don't bother switching the light on. I down the rest of my own bourbon and stand my glass beside Natalie's.

I go to her and pull her into my arms. My lips find hers and it's like my kiss breathes life into her. She wraps her arms around me, her hands running up and down my back. Her mouth is hungry for me, her tongue probing into my mouth as her hands make their way beneath my shirt.

I run my hands down Natalie's body, feeling the curve of her hips. I move one hand between us and rub my fingers over her mound. She's wearing loose fitting trousers, but she still moans at my touch. She presses herself tighter against my hand, moving her hips slightly.

She pulls her mouth from mine and kisses down my face, over my jaw and down my neck. Her kisses bring goose bumps to the surface of my skin. She steps back from me and begins to unbutton my shirt. She pulls it down my arms and lets it drop to the floor and then she looks me up and down. She nods approvingly when she sees my abs and I bite my lip to stop myself from smirking.

She runs her nails lightly over my chest and I increase the pressure on her mound. I lean in and kiss her again, walking her backwards towards my bed. When her legs hit the mattress, she breaks our kiss long enough to kick her heels off, hop up onto the bed and scoot backwards. I join her eagerly, wanting to get her out of those clothes, to taste her pussy.

Our lips lock again as I reach down and begin to open her trousers. I have barely gotten the button open when my cell phone rings loudly in my pocket, making us both jump.

"Ignore it," Natalie breathes.

Like I was going to do anything else. She finishes opening her trousers and pushes them down, kicking them away. Her legs have a light tan, and they're every bit as long as I imagined them to be. I trail my fingers up one of her inner thighs. I run my fingers over her panties, feeling the clinging dampness of them. Oh she wants me alright. I push her panties to one side and slip my fingers inside of her lips. My cock hardens as I feel how wet she is. How ready for me.

Natalie gasps as my fingers find her clit. I begin to work her, listening to her gasps as I bring her close to the edge. My cell phone rings again.

"Goddammit," I shout, pulling my hand away from Natalie and slamming my fist down on the mattress between us in frustration.

I pull my phone out of my pocket, ready to cut the call off and turn the damned thing off. It's Matt, my older brother. It has to be important for him to be calling at this hour. He's not going to quit calling until I answer, and if I ignore him, he'll start on the landline.

"Fuck," I say quietly.

Natalie grabs my hand and tries to move it back down to her pussy. I pull it away gently.

"I'm sorry. I have to take this. It's my brother and he wouldn't call at this time if it wasn't something important. Make yourself comfortable, I won't be a minute," I tell her.

I jump up off the bed, trying to ignore my erection as it presses uncomfortably against my trousers. I can hear Natalie sighing as I leave the room. I pull the door closed behind me. I know how she feels, but I plan on getting this call over with quickly and then making it up to her.

"What?" I demand as I take the call in the hallway.

"Charming," Matt laughs.

"I'm kind of busy here. What do you want?"

"Well seeing as you brought it up, what I want is for you to stop fucking potential clients Seb. Jeez. Can you not just keep it in your fucking pants for once?"

Apparently I can thanks to him.

"I don't know what you're talking about," I say.

"Sure you don't. This could blow the whole deal," Matt says.

I can hear the irritation in his voice. It should be me who is irritated. I'm the one getting disturbed.

"Don't worry about that bro. The only thing getting blown here tonight will be me. If you ever get off the damned phone that is."

"Do you have to be so crude?"

"Yup."

"Look I get that you think with your cock, but this is an important deal Seb," Matt says.

I'm getting annoyed now. Matt knows I would never do anything that would negatively affect the business.

"Look it's not like I dragged her here kicking and screaming. She made it quite clear she was interested," I say.

"Yeah? And what happens when she finds out you're not interested in anything other than one night with her?"

"Oh trust me. She'll have had that good a time that she won't hold it against me."

Matt sighs loudly.

"Can you just be serious for one moment? You're putting the deal in jeopardy and you know it. And for what? A cheap lay you won't even remember this time next week."

His judgemental tone hits my last nerve.

"You're one to talk Matt. If I remember correctly, and I know I do, it was only a year or so ago that you almost allowed a fucking criminal who was stealing from us to walk free because you started to think with your cock instead of your head."

"That was different," Matt snaps.

"How? Because you were the one fucking up?"

"No. Because Callie wasn't just a conquest to me. I had real feelings for her."

"And how do you know I don't have feelings for Natalie?"

"Do you?"

"Well no, but that's not the point I'm making."

"So what is your point?"

"My point is that I'm perfectly capable of keeping business and pleasure separate. Natalie and I are both adults and this won't affect the deal. Now if you'll excuse me, I've got a horny and pissed off woman waiting for me."

"Wait," Matt says. "There is one other thing."

There's something in the way he says it that piques my interest and instead of cutting off the call as I had planned to, I hear myself sigh and ask him what it is.

"Well it's something I know you'll be very interested to hear. But it's clear you're otherwise engaged so maybe I'll just tell you later," he teases me.

Now I'm really fucking intrigued. What could Matt know that he clearly wants so badly to tell me that he's winding me up this way at one one o'clock instead of being in bed with Callie?

"Just spit it out," I say.

"What about Natalie? Isn't she waiting for you?"

Natalie who?

"She can wait another couple of minutes."

"Kimberley is back in town," Matt says.

The playful tone is gone from his voice and I know he's serious. The news hits me like a brick wall and I am momentarily mute. I find my voice eventually and I croak out a what, but it's too late. Matt has hung up and I am left with the buzzing noise of a dead line in my ear.

I freeze on the spot, the phone still glued to my ear although there's no one on the other end. Kimberley is back in town. How? Why? When? I have so many questions. I can't believe Matt dropped that bombshell on me and then hung up. I finally peel the phone away from my ear, and call Matt, but the call goes straight to his voicemail. He's turned his phone off, just like I knew he would.

I curse and throw my cell phone to the ground. Kimberley is back in town. It plays on a loop in my head as I picture the girl I once knew. She was stunning with flaming red hair and piercing green eyes. She had this laugh, a gentle musical sound that was so infectious that anyone around her would automatically laugh with her.

I haven't seen her in like four years, but the vision of her is still as fresh in my mind as it was the day she ... Never mind. I'm not going to let myself go there. So Kimberley is back in town? So what?

I hear a door open behind me and I jump. I turn around and see Natalie standing in the doorway to my bedroom. Fuck. I had forgotten she was even here. I can't do this with her. Not now. My erection is long gone, and Natalie won't be the one to bring my cock back to life tonight. I just want her gone.

"Is everything ok?" she purrs.

"Something came up," I say, pleased that my voice comes out even. "I'm sorry, but you're going to have to leave."

"Leave?" she repeats, frowning at me.

She sounds pissed off and I don't blame her, but I can't do anything about it now. I can't bring myself to even look at her, let alone fuck her. Kimberley is back in town.

"Yeah," I say.

She smiles. That seductive smile that a few hours ago, hell a few minutes ago, was driving me wild. Now it only irritates me. Is she deaf or what? Why won't she just go away?

"Or I could wait in your bedroom until you've fixed whatever crisis has come up. I'll keep the bed warm and give you something to look forward to," she says.

She runs her tongue over her lips and I feel nothing.

"For fuck sake Natalie. Take a hint. We're done here. Just get out," I snap.

Her face changes from seductive to shocked and then angry.

"You absolute asshole," she snaps.

She storms back into my bedroom and for a moment, I think she's still not planning to leave, but then I remember her stripping off her trousers. I'm not going to insist she leaves half naked.

I stand in the hallway, still rooted to the spot. I hear Natalie huffing as she grabs her trousers. She comes back into the hallway with them pressed against her front, her shoes dangling from her hand by her side.

I can see tears shining in her eyes. I don't think she's that upset. I think she's angry and humiliated, and I wish I could make it better, I really do, but I can't. Anything I say now is only going to make this worse. I keep my mouth shut as she stalks closer to me.

"You really are a first class fuck boy," she snarls.

I shrug. What is there to say to that? It's not like she's wrong, and it's not like she didn't know that when she came back here with me. She just didn't care when she thought she was going to get her way with me.

I don't say any of that to her. I don't want to argue with her. I just want her gone. I can smell her perfume and now it doesn't smell sweet like I thought it did earlier. It's over powering. Nauseating.

She's still making no move to leave.

"Well? Don't you have anything to say for yourself?" she demands.

"Close the door on your way out," I say.

Her mouth drops open and she shakes her head.

"Wow. Just fucking wow," she says in a low voice that bristles with anger.

She finally starts to walk away from me. She reaches the top of the stairs and turns back to me. I can see the venom in her expression, the embarrassment in her flushed cheeks.

"You should know I don't do business with people who are unreliable. The deal is off Sebastian. Don't bother calling me."

Dammit. That's what Matt said would happen. But then again, he was the one who dropped that bombshell on me. What did he think would happen after that? I have no idea, but I know I have to fix this. I'll give her some sob story, make her feel sorry for me. Maybe I'll even promise to make it up to her at the weekend when my head isn't reeling.

"Kimberley wait," I say, taking a step forwards.

"Did you just call me Kimberley?" Natalie demands.

Fuck. I did. I know I did. There goes any chance I had of rectifying this.

"Natalie," I say, still not quite ready to give up without at least trying to turn the situation around.

"Fuck you," she says.

She starts down the stairs. I hear her running down the hallway at the bottom and then I hear the front door open and slam closed. I don't bother going after her. What's the point? The deal is off. I screwed up big time. And Kimberley is back in town.

I take a step backwards and my back hits the wall. I slowly slide down it and sit on the ground, my knees drawn up and my elbows resting on them. I run my hands over my face and try to make sense of the swirl of bottomless emotions that flood through me.

Kimberley is back in town.

Chapter Thirty-Two

CHAPTER 2

Sebastian

I've been trying to call Matt for the last hour, but his phone keeps going straight to voicemail. I've called his office and his secretary insisted he was in a meeting. I know that's bullshit. I could hear it in her voice. He's avoiding my calls on purpose.

Well he's not going to be able to avoid me in person. Screw what his secretary has to say. I'm going to have this out with Matt right now. I step out of the elevator and stalk along the corridor. A few associates run back and forth going about their day like the whole world hasn't just been turned upside down. I return their nods, their good morning greetings. It's anything but a good morning, but I remind myself how I let my own emotions screw up a deal last night and I keep myself in control now. I don't want to take my foul mood out on the staff here.

My head is banging from the alcohol last night and the lack of sleep. I was expecting that but I was expecting it to be for a very different reason. The sort of reason that makes the pain bearable.

I move through the open plan centre of the floor, trying to ignore the way the low hubbub of voices pierces my head. Even the sound of computer keys clicking sets my jaw on edge. I reach into my pocket and pull out a strip of painkillers. I dry swallow two and tell myself they're working.

"Rough night?" Bradley, one of our top accountants, grins when he sees me popping the pills.

I bite my tongue to stop myself from snapping at him that it's none of his business. Bradley and I go way back and we've always had an easy relationship, more like friends than a boss and a worker. Any other day I would have laughed and regaled him with stories of the wild night I'd had last night.

"You could say that," I reply, forcing a laugh.

He pulls his desk drawer open and hands me a sealed bottle of ice cold water. I'm glad now I didn't bite his head off.

"Thanks," I say as I open the top and drink half of the bottle down in one go.

The cool water revives me somewhat and I don't know if the pills are kicking in quickly or if I was just dehydrated, but the pain in my head begins to recede, becoming a dull ache rather than a sharp pain. I sit down on the edge of Bradley's desk.

"How's the report coming along?" I ask.

"It's looking good," Bradley says. "I'll have it over to you by the end of today officially, but unofficially, I've been through Benton's books with a fine tooth comb and they're a good investment. They're financially strong, and with a few tweaks, they could be a real cash cow."

I nod thoughtfully. Bradley is right. I knew it from a quick glance over the figures, but I wanted to do due diligence and be certain there were no skeletons lurking in their books before I began the negotiations. They're due to get underway in the next week or so.

I feel better about Natalie suddenly. Her company was small fry compared to Benton's. And if we pull off the Benton merger successfully, no one will give a shit about Natalie. Not even my father.

"Nice work," I say to Bradley who beams under my praise. "Dot the I's and cross the T's and get the report to me by lunch time and take the rest of the day off."

"Thanks Sebastian," he says, clearly taken aback.

I laugh and pat him on the shoulder before moving on towards Matt's office. I feel a little calmer and more in control of myself as I reach Matt's secretary's desk, but I'm still in no mood to be fobbed off.

"Morning Sheila," I say, not stopping.

"Mr Hunter doesn't want to be disturbed," she says, jumping up and standing between me and the office door.

"Ah come on now," I say, giving her my most charming smile. "You know that doesn't include visits from his baby brother."

She blushes a little and smiles.

"Well ummm, let me go check with him," she says.

That's the confirmation I needed that he's not with a client. I side step around her and put my hand on the door handle.

"No need," I grin, slipping inside before she can do anything else to try and stop me.

She hurries in behind me.

"I'm sorry Mr Hunter, I ..."

"It's ok," Matt cuts her off.

"Right. Thank you. And sorry again. Would you like some refreshments?" Sheila stammers.

"No thank you. Sebastian won't be staying," Matt says.

He aims the comment at me. I just smirk at him until Sheila leaves the room pulling the door closed behind her. As the door closes, my smirk fades and I march towards Matt's desk, ready to demand to know why he's dodging my calls. Before I can speak, he looks at me disapprovingly.

"You look tired Seb. Late night last night?" he says.

Everyone is a damned comedian it seems.

"Funny. Why the hell are you dodging my calls?" I demand.

"Because I had nothing to say to you. I owe you none of my time Seb. Your actions last night have caused us to lose a client. Natalie Graham called this morning and made it clear we won't be getting her business."

"And who's fault is that?" I say.

"Umm yours," Matt says, raising an eyebrow.

"Yeah I'm pretty sure I'm not the one who interrupted us with a phone call. Let's just say after that, the mood was kind of ruined."

"I wonder why that was," Matt says.

I ignore the jibe. This is nothing to do with Kimberley. This is about the business.

"You accused me of putting my personal life above the business, and now you're dodging my calls in work time because you're annoyed that I called off a one night stand?"

"I'm annoyed that you put yourself in a position to lose us business," Matt counters.

I shrug and sit down in the seat opposite his.

"Whatever," I say. "Natalie's business was a drop in the ocean compared to the Benton merger. I was calling you to see how close we are to getting the first meetings set up. Bradley has just about finished up the financial report and everything is looking as good as we hoped it would."

"We're almost there. The preliminary talks have gone well and we're looking to get started early next week," Matt says. He grins. "But you know all of that. So why don't you tell me what you really want."

"That was what I really wanted. To call you out on ignoring my calls," I lie.

"Ok, I hear you loud and clear. So if that's it then, I've kind of got work to do," Matt says.

I can tell by the gleam in his eye he knows why I'm really here. I mean sure I was annoyed at him dodging my calls, but he's right. I didn't need to ask about the Benton merger. I knew all of that. And if the meetings got pushed forward, of course someone would have reached out to me and let me know. I'm annoyed at him for dodging my calls because I wanted to ask him about one thing. Her. Kimberley.

I eye Matt as I try to work out a way to bring the conversation around to Kimberley without it being obvious I've thought of nothing but her all damned night. His lips curl up slightly at the corners and I know he's enjoying my discomfort. I suppose this is his pay back for all the times I've embarrassed him over the years with new girlfriends. And for all the flirting I do with his fiancé, Callie.

I don't want to give him the satisfaction of asking him for more details about Kimberley, but I know I can't just get up and walk out of here without hearing everything there is to know about her return. I look down into my lap.

"Is it true what you said last night? Is Kimberley really back in town?" I say.

Matt doesn't answer immediately and I force myself to look up and meet his eye. His amused look pisses me off but I bite my tongue, waiting for an answer.

"It's true," he says.

I feel a mixture of emotions flood me. I'm happy to hear that she's back, and at the same time, I'm apprehensive to know that I might run into her. I am also fuming that she's made no effort to contact me. But then why would she after what happened between us?

"Have you seen her?" I ask.

Matt seems to be determined to make me ask the questions to get the information from him, even though he must know it's killing me to have to practically beg him for the information.

"Yeah I've seen her. I ran into her a couple of days ago. She looks good Seb. Damned good. She still has that shock of red hair; it's right down almost to her ass now. And she's filled out in all of the right places if you get my drift."

Oh I get his drift alright. My cock is twitching just thinking about Kimberley all grown up.

"She's really grown into herself. She's beautiful now," Matt says.

"She was always beautiful," I say before I can stop myself.

Matt grins at my words.

"But then all of the women I sleep with are beautiful," I add, more for my own benefit than his.

If I thought he was going to let me save face that easily, I was sorely mistaken. He is most definitely enjoying my discomfort. He nods, an exaggerated nod.

"Yeah I'm sure they are, but not like Kimberley. She's ... something else," he says.

"Maybe I should be calling up Callie and telling her she's got competition," I say.

Matt laughs.

"I don't think she'd be even close to how jealous you are right now," he says. "About our chat I mean."

"You spoke to her?" I say, again ignoring his jibe.

"Sure," Matt says. "I told you I ran into her. What did you think I did? Just ignored her?"

I shrug. I hadn't thought that for a minute, but I just wanted to find out what they had to talk about without having to come out and ask, but Matt pauses again, clearly waiting for me to ask. God sometimes I really fucking hate Matt. He loves to watch me squirm and today is no exception.

"So how is she? What's she up to?" I ask, doing my best to sound like I'm just making casual conversation.

"You seem awfully interested in her," Matt says.

"She's an old friend. Why wouldn't I be interested in how she's doing?" I ask.

"You weren't interested when I told you I ran into Bobby St Clair a couple of weeks ago."

"Who?"

"Exactly. You don't even remember half of the people you used to know. But Kimberley ..."

"Is different," I finish.

My small confession softens Matt slightly and he begins to tell me about their run in without me having to keep digging for more.

"She's good. She's done well for herself. She's the CFO at a big company. She's in town on business actually. She's staying at the Hilton on Mercer Way. She always did like her luxuries. And now she's living the jet-setter lifestyle. She's just got back from a three month tour of Europe. Rome, Paris, Madrid, Prague. You name it, she's been there."

"Sounds like she's really made it," I say.

"Yeah she has. You should see her tan. She was glowing," Matt adds,

There's one more thing I want to ask, but I am afraid of the answer. I think I know the answer. Kimberley was never really the settling down and getting married type, but people change. I've changed. Maybe she has too. I have to know.

"So does she have any kids?" I ask, skirting around the topic.

"Kimberley the workaholic with a kid? Are you kidding me?" Matt laughs.

Despite myself, I find myself laughing along with him. Nothing about Kimberley says maternal. She never hated children, she just hated the idea of having her own. Being tied to a tiny human instead of a desk was never her idea of a life she wanted.

"It was a dumb question," I admit.

And not at all the one I wanted to ask.

"I wonder how her partner feels about her aversion to kids," I say.

I was going for casual, but I can hear the tremor in my voice as I say it and I know Matt must hear it too.

"She hasn't got a partner currently. And when she finds one, she's not exactly backwards in coming forwards. I'm sure she'll make it known early enough in the relationship that if it's a deal breaker, the guy can flee."

"Yeah," I laugh. "Kimberley doesn't hold back. If she wants something, then everyone knows it. And equally if she doesn't want something then everyone knows it."

Like when she no longer wanted me.

I push the thought aside, concentrating instead on the joy of hearing that she's not taken. Not that it matters. I'm well and truly over Kimberley and I don't want to go back there. Not even a little bit. I was just curious that's all.

I try to convince myself my thoughts are true. It's hard work, but I think if I tell myself it often enough, I can start to believe it. Because no matter what happens, no matter what old feelings hearing Kimberley's name stirs up inside of me, it's in the past. She's in the past. And I won't risk going there again.

Please pre-order the book here:
Untangle My Heart.

ABOUT THE AUTHOR

Thank you so much for reading!
If you have enjoyed the book and would like to leave a
precious review for me, please kindly do so here.

Reckless Entanglement

Please click on the link below to receive info about my latest
releases and giveaways.
NEVER MISS A THING

Or
come and say hello here:

ALSO BY IONA ROSE

Nanny Wanted

CEO's Secret Baby

New Boss, Old Enemy

Craving The CEO

Forbidden Touch

Crushing On My Doctor

Made in the USA
Las Vegas, NV
06 May 2022

48466887R00148